Mary of the Mayflower

Mary of the Mayflower

Written and Illustrated by

Diane Stevenson Stone

Direct Descendant of Mary Chilton

Diane Stevenson Stone

ISBN 978-0-9895523-1-8
Cover image: "Landing of the Pilgrims" 1877 by Henry A. Bacon
Courtesy of Pilgrim Hall Museum

Although inspired by historical events and actual persons, this novel is a work of fiction. While care has been taken to remain true to the historical and cultural setting, many details have been changed for dramatic purposes, and many things, including certain conversations, dialogue, motivations, and actions, are purely the creation of the author.

Printed in the United States of America

Publishing services provided by Scrivener Books
info@scrivenerbooks.com
First Edition

Cover, text, and internal art © Diane Stevenson Stone
Edited by Heidi Brockbank
Typeset by Heather Justesen

Cover image: "Landing of the Pilgrims," an original painting by Henry A. Bacon, painted in 1877, depicting Mary Chilton leaping onto Plymouth Rock. The author has secured the rights from Ann Berry, executive director of the Pilgrim Hall Museum, to reproduce the cover and in this book.

Dedication

To my children,
Jennifer Stone McKay, Patricia Stone, Thomas Leslie Stone,
John David Stone, Jared Walker Stone, Emily Stone,
Sarah Lucy Stone Lovell, and Peter Kimball Stone.
&
To the children of all Americans
whose forefathers came,
early or late,
as Pilgrims to a new land,
America.

Acknowledgments

I wish to thank my father, Stanley Walker Stevenson, who laid important groundwork for my book. With his love of our forefathers as well as his curious and eager research, his spirit of genealogy continues on to the next generation. Thank you to my immediate family and grandchildren, who have read earlier drafts and given me encouragement and support from the very start. Karen Sedgwick Stone, my remarkable sister-in-law, patiently read one of my many drafts and gave me important insights. Later, my dear sister, Kathleen Stevenson Lange, who knows and loves children's literature, read my manuscript and rooted me on. Sarah Stevenson Johnson read through the entire manuscript and gave valuable input. Before I even knew how to use a computer, my friend, Jennifer Robertson, with an eye for detail, typed every word. Phuong Scalf, a young Vietnamese student with her military husband, Sam, read my final rough draft and then typed a more complete copy, carefully dropping into the text my pen-and-ink illustrations.

A special thank-you to respected creative professional Kieth Merrill for his generous comments in the foreword. And to Ann Berry, executive director of the Pilgrim Hall Museum in Plymouth, Massachusetts, for permitting me to use the image of Henry A. Bacon's painting, *The Landing of the Pilgrims*. My appreciation goes to author Jerry Borrowman, who took time to introduce me to Eschler Editing, who, in turn, guided me through every step of the way. Also, thanks to Heather Justesen, who made magic with the typesetting and the arrangement of my art work; JJ Robinson, a gifted graphic artist who created an amazing cover; and Chris Bigelow, whose professional knowledge as owner of Scrivener Books helped make this book possible.

I am especially indebted to Heidi Brockbank, project manager and editor at Eschler Editing. She has been my mentor and close advisor during months of editing and provided an excellent perspective and a complete understanding of the historical genre of my manuscript. Her expertise has been invaluable.

Finally, to my beloved husband, Tom Stone, who is a valued resource and my constant support—for helping me to keep my head above water and lovingly encouraging me through to the end of each one of my creative projects.

Foreword

Ralph Waldo Emerson wrote, "We are the children of many sires, and every drop of blood in us, in its turn, betrays its ancestors."

Diane Stevenson Stone has written an engaging historical fiction about one of her many ancestors who was part of the larger group of brave people who set out as passengers on the *Mayflower* to seek religious freedom.

Much has been written in greater detail about this courageous journey to the New World. Diane's purpose of this book is to tell a little known yet pivotal moment in our nation's history. Through her creative imagination, and from careful research, she strives to write of the sacrifice, friendships made, class relationships, the anguish, humor and faith, so that we might understand more fully how to cherish and maintain the ideals of our American freedom by catching the very spirit and purity of purpose of our Pilgrim Fathers.

The story begins in Amsterdam, Holland, in the warm Chilton family kitchen, where young, spunky Mary questions her mother about being English. Early on, Mary discovers a wise yet ominous inscription in her locket left by her grandmother. At great risk Mary's family eventually faces unknown dangers on the voyage of the *Mayflower*—revealing for the first time intimate details of everyday life aboard the *Mayflower* that could mean the difference between life and death. It is an enticing story for young people. Life for Mary is a sober adventure filled with new emotions from deep despair to sustaining hope.

Diane loves telling this story with passion and pride, gratitude, and with a certain delight that the same blood that ran through

Mary's veins also runs through hers. She says with a twinkle in her eyes, "That's the Mary Chilton in me."

This vivid account, full of surprising twists and turns, is relevant to today's experience while also historically accurate and believable. It is about a girl who manages, in the male-dominated society of 1620, to shape and create her own course.

–Kieth W. Merrill, writer, director, and producer
    Academy Award–winning American filmmaker

Table of Contents

Chapter 1
The Heirloom

"I'M A DUTCH GIRL."

Mary's mother quickly replied, "No, Mary, ye are English."

"Aye, we've come from England but we live in a Dutch country," her father proudly added, stirring the embers in the hearth.

"But I feel like I'm a Dutch girl and I look like I'm Dutch. How can I be English and feel so Dutch?" Mary wondered as she sat on a tall stool, petting her newly found cat.

Mother wiped off a carrot with her apron and handed it to Mary. Leaning into her, she said, "Mary, there is so much for ye to know and understand about who ye are and where ye came from, dear."

Mother returned to chopping vegetables. "Mary, because ye are the youngest in our family, ye don't remember, like your older sisters do, when we lived in England and had to leave our home to travel to Holland." It was true. Mary had been little more than a toddler. All she could recall of those dark days were a few hazy memories. Trying to remember always left her feeling a little sad, like she'd lost a good friend whose face and name she couldn't remember.

From the rafters overhead hung bundles of dried herbs, nets of onions, and a basketful of eggs while the warm firelight from the hearth flickered over everything without distinction, including Mary's puzzled face.

Mary scooped up her cat, whose name was "Master Albert," just in time before he upset a basket filled with colored skeins of wool yarn which sat on the sill of the window facing the alley.

She climbed onto her father's lap. "How old was I when we came here?" Mary studied her father's reflective[1] face.

"Ye were a wee child, so small that when we arrived in Holland in the middle of the night, ye thought the windmills were scary giants."

Mary giggled. She loved hearing her father talk about when she was smaller.

"What else, Father?" Mary moved her fingers through Master Albert's warm, fluffy fur. She listened as her father's rich voice began, always learning something new from him.

"Mary," her mother interrupted with concern, "If ye handle poor Mister Albert too much . . . ."

"His name is *Master* Albert, Mum, not Mister!"

"Fair enough, dear. I just do not want him to get sick," continued her mother.

Master Albert's green eyes and soft golden fur fascinated Mary. She had found him on her way home one afternoon in a nearby alley, sniffing for food.

Father pulled her close. "When ye were just a wee little girl, we lived in a small corner of Canterbury, England. Engle and Isabella, being the oldest daughters, helped Mum in the cottage. She taught them to be temperate[2] and chaste,[3] to tend a garden, and prepare food. And ye spent much time in my tailor shop."

---

[1] **Reflective:** serious, thoughtful
[2] **Temperate:** moderate, self-restrained in action, speech
[3] **Chaste:** pure, decent, modest, simple in style, not ornate

"I do remember folks coming to ye for clothes," Mary responded.

"Do ye remember that?" He went on. "Ye have a good memory. Aye, ye would greet them with cheerful smiles, and ye were full of life to the brim. I think back on how ye would hurry to complete your little tasks, twisting skeins[4] of wool and colored spools of thread and gathering up the scraps of fabric from the floor, and straightening the precious packets of needles. Then ye would tug on me apron and eagerly plead in your small voice, 'Father, may I go now?'" Her father mimicked Mary's little voice.

Mary put her head on his chest and giggled.

"Ye were such good company for me. I would always glance around the shop for more things to keep ye busy hoping to find a reason for ye to stay longer."

Listening eagerly, she sat up with a big smile. "And did ye keep me there longer?"

Father tapped her nose lightly. "If ye had finished your chores I'd send ye on your way."

"Where would I go?" She wanted to know everything.

"Ye were never idle. Ye loved to play in the dell[5] where the ground was hilly and hummocky.[6] Ye would burst out the door to meet your jolly pals. I watched thee skip past the gatepost, across the fields of bluebells and into the woods. Do ye remember those little blue flowers?"

Mary squinted her eyes and shook her head, trying to

---

[4] **Skein:** a quantity of thread or yarn in a coil
[5] **Dell:** meadow
[6] **Hummocky:** a low rounded hill; knoll

remember. Somewhere in the back of her mind she caught a glimpse of sunshine and a flash of blue.

On a strand of silk cord around her neck, Mary wore a golden locket engraved with roses and an old inscription: "Sweet are the uses of adversity."[7] It had been handed down in the family from her beloved grandmother Isabelle. The family remembered her fondly as Nana.

"Father, tell me more about Nana." Mary loved this time with her parents, when she was the only one at home with no sisters around to divide or share their attention.

"Oh, Mary, she was a fine woman with great courage. She died many years before ye were born and the locket that ye wear is an heirloom that belonged to her. "

"Was she very old when she died?" Mary asked.

"Aye, but let me continue." His eyes held a faraway look, as if he were lost in thought as he spoke lovingly of her grandmother. "She had a soft voice and bright blue eyes just like yours, Mary."

Until then, Mary had never given any thought to what color her eyes were. With no looking glass to catch a glimpse, no one ever knew what, or even who, they might resemble.

"Why did she die?" Mary wondered.

Her father paused. "Well, she was old for her years because Nana endured many hardships and carried heavy burdens. Her greatest desire was to serve her family. She had dreams of a better time and place for her children and grandchildren."

He continued, "Whenever I smell fresh lavender, I think of her. She would gather long stems in her arms and weave them together to adorn our humble cottage. While she was a very strong woman

---

[7] **Adversity:** misfortune or troubled state

with a lot of responsibility, there was a kind gentleness about her. I wish you could have known her."

Holding up her locket, Mary asked her father, "Tell me again what it says on my locket." Like most women and girls, Mary didn't know how to read or write. Of course, not many men could read either, unless they were noblemen or scholars or priests. Mary was glad to have a father learned enough to be able to read the Bible to the family.

Now her father turned the locket over and read out loud. "Sweet are the uses of adversity. It is a wise and yet foreboding[8] message. Family members who came before our time affect us now. What they believed, their choices, and the way they lived their lives has a direct influence on others for many generations."

Master Albert leaped away as Mary slipped down off her father's lap. She didn't understand all that he was saying, but she knew his voice sounded serious. She felt a slight chill run through her body, wondering what hardships life might bring.

Mary studied her locket, wondering aloud, "How can adversity be sweet?" Even at her young age, she was aware of some of the sorrows life brought. Although it was seldom mentioned, she knew that she had seven siblings that had died before she was born. Only her two sisters and she survived. Maybe that's why she always felt a little sad when she tried to remember what life had been like in England. How could something that brought such pain be sweet? She shrugged her shoulders. "Maybe someday I'll know what it means."

Her mother quietly added, "Trust the inscription on your locket, and one day ye will better understand the meaning. Everybody's life has some adversity. 'Tis what ye do with it that makes all the difference."

---

[8] **Foreboding:** to have a bad feeling about something

Just then Master Albert suddenly jumped up on the table where Mum was preparing food! "Scat, scat, go away! Mary, ye must domesticate this animal! He may be a master but he is NOT master of my kitchen!"

Chapter 2
Escape

MASTER CHILTON ROSE FROM his chair and walked to the little inset window. Pulling the lace curtain aside, he looked down the slight footpath called Grachtengordel Canal Alley. Grachtengordel meant "narrow ditch," and the alley was as small and cramped as the canal that ran parallel to the path. It was getting dark, and he was expecting his older daughters. At night, Mary's sisters returned home along a dingy, ill-lit passageway. It was a distressed section of Amsterdam, but it was where they could afford housing along with many other of their congregation members. Together they renamed their narrow alley "Gezelligheid," which meant cozy or pleasant.

The oldest Chilton daughters made swiftly down the alley with their workbaskets in hand to their small home and cozy fire. By keeping to the narrow byways and alleys, they avoided the wet wind from the rooftops. They closed out the noisy city behind them as they entered their humble place of rest. Engle and Isabella were always relieved to return home from their long days of tediously working needles and thread into fine lace for the rich ladies of Amsterdam to wear on their cuffs and collars when they attended weddings, the baptisms of their infants, fine affairs, and even funerals. The Chilton sisters had a reputation for creating beautiful lace, and their customers were demanding and expected the finest.

"Come along and warm thyselves by the fire and have something hot!" Mary's mother stirred the pottage of herring,[9] while her father carried the coal and short supply of chopped wood to keep the hearth fire burning.

Master Albert ran up beside them, paused to lick his paws, stretched, and then darted off again. In the evenings, the rafters would ring with songs and light laughter, filling the small dwelling that was squeezed between the dark alleyways of the big city.

It was the middle of another cold winter, and they were chilled to the bone until the fire was underway as they gathered in the kitchen, which was their main room and where they could keep warm.

Father was a talented tailor and benevolent to all that knew him. He worked hard to support his family. After a modest meal, Mary's family talked of their day's work. Mary liked to see her father's gentle face as he reached for the old family Bible where it was always kept up on the mantel. He began reading aloud from the pages, while everyone found their place near the open fire.

While father was reading, the cat, who had come back to sit on Mary's lap, darted away from her. When she gave a shiver and reached down to pull her stockings up, she was distracted just long enough that Master Albert's allegiance went to Engle. He crossed the room and settled next to her by the fireplace hearth. Mary was too content to feel abandoned. This was one of her favorite times of the evening. Mary loved listening to the stories of faithful men and women. It struck her that they had all faced adversity: Esther putting

---

[9] **Herring:** a small fish of the North Atlantic

her life in danger to save her people; Sarah waiting endless years to have a child; Ruth leaving her home to travel to a distant country. Would she have been that brave?

Father closed the sacred book. "Let me see how well ye know your poem," he told Mary and her older sisters. "'Tis six lines. Who can say them by heart?"

With rapid response Mary recited the poem she'd learned since she first began to talk:

The Bible, a book of worth.
Bound carefully by leather girth.
Held by Father's hand since birth.
Gives life purpose here on earth.
'Tis musty, worn, tattered, and old.
'Twas owned by God, so I've been told.

She gave her father a hug, and his soft beard brushed across her rosy cheeks.

He whispered in her ear, "Mary, those are prudent words you have committed to memory."

Mary was pleased at her father's praise. In that fleeting moment, peaceful and secure in his arms, she knew that she was loved and treasured, not only as her father's daughter, but as a child of God.

In spite of chores that never seemed to be done, the family gathered around the hearth. Engle brushed her long hair, Isabella knitted woolen stockings, and Mary watched her mother's nimble fingers mending cloth. Mary carefully copied every move, trying to make her own stitches as neat and small as her mother's. Mother kept her needle moving deftly as she cheerfully said, "Come, let us have a tune."

Master Albert found his favorite spot and curled up next to the fire. One by one they began to sing a favorite hymn.

All praise to Thee my God this night,
For all the blessings of the light.
Keep me, oh, keep me, King of Kings
Beneath Thine own almighty wings.

"Father," Isabella spoke softly, "will ye tell us stories about when we lived in England?"

"Goodwife, do we have time to speak of our homeland this evening?" Father had a twinkle in his eye.

Mary's mother responded, "Aye, there's enough time before bed."

The girls loved hearing stories of their homeland, especially Mary, who recalled so little. She sank to the floor wide-eyed, with her chin nestled on her knees as her father began to speak.

"Those were laborious[10] days and nights." Father sighed.

"We learned that the king's men had punished some folks in a nearby hamlet.[11] One woman did not baptize her baby and was told the infant would be condemned; they forced the woman off to prison. In another cottage across the meadow, a father was dragged away, clinging to his goodwife, because he spoke openly about religious freedom: 'If all men are equal before God,' he spoke bravely, 'why not before the law!' No one ever saw him again."

"Where did he go?" Mary asked in a worried whisper.

"Shh, Mary, ye must listen," bid[12] her mother. At once Mary held her tongue. She knew that children should be still and quiet.

---

[10] **Laborious:** difficult
[11] **Hamlet:** a very small village
[12] **Bid:** to be commanded; ordered

But sometimes the feelings in her heart threatened to spill over, and often, the words just burst out of Mary without warning. In spite of her curiosity, Father seldom reprimanded her. He loved all his daughters, but as his last child born, Mary held a special place in his heart. Indeed, she was the darling even of her sisters and mother—a bright, cheerful child who was still young and least burdened by everyday life and household chores.

Thoughtfully, he proceeded. "Few people would speak up like that. Instead, they would hide in their farm houses and cottages, fearful of King James. We realized we no longer had freedom to worship as we saw fit and knew that we had to separate from the king's church, so we gathered with others who called themselves Separatists."[13]

Mary was watching both her mother and father closely and wanted to ask more questions, but she didn't say a word or budge. She sat quietly with Isabella and Engle. All three of them leaned in as they listened intently.

"It was the first time the king's men had come unannounced. Our settlement had been awakened in the wee hours of the morning by sounds of horses. A cool wind moved through the meadow grass and down in the dell. It had been a chilly night. Lanterns were lit a few flickers at a time. One by one, folks peered out of their dark windows. There were sharp, angry shouts through the narrow streets." The girls loved how their father told stories, but they knew that this was more than just a story.

"If ye will not bow to the crown, off to the stocks[14] ye will go!"

---

[13] **Separatist:** those who separated themselves because of their beliefs from the oppression of King James and the mandated religion of England—also called Puritans and Pilgrims

[14] **Stocks:** a wooden frame with holes for confining the ankles or wrists, formerly used for punishment

They enjoyed how their father used his deep voice to add emotion and suspense to the life's experience he was sharing.

"Children peeped out from the corners of the garden gate, and others ran into their parents' arms. Families held on tight to each other and all that was precious. Commotion was stirring within every humble household. One old, God-fearing neighbor spoke to Mother in a low, trembling whisper. 'The township of Dewsbury has seen countless travesties. There is talk of farms being burned to the ground and scores of innocent folks and even children beheaded for refusing to bow to the royal crown. What on earth will we do?'"

Mary could hardly sit still thinking of how unfair the world around them could be. She beckoned Master Albert to come sit in her lap.

Mother said, "Mary, ye dashed to your sisters for protection. Even though Engle and Isabella were frightened as well, they kept calm and gathered you about." Her mother's voice was tender and soft, but her face was grim. She leaned over and rested her hand reassuringly on Mary's head. "The three of ye held each other close."

Mary had so many questions, but she kept her head down trying to be still because she knew children did not speak until they were spoken to. Once she recalled her father telling them, "If ye do all of the talking, you will tell everything ye know, and soon ye won't know anything."

"My good husband," Mother began slowly, "remember the many funerals? The king . . ." For a moment, Mother paused, then in a trembling voice, she said, "The king had put dear friends to death by hanging or worse." Her words had fallen to a whisper.

"No need to whisper," father reassured her. "The Dutch gave

asylum[15] to the British and we are safe here in Holland; we can speak as freely as we wish."

With obvious pain in her voice, Mother said, "With our family living so far away in the English countryside, I thought they would leave us alone."

"Now goodwife, calm yourself. That time is past and over. We need not worry." Mary's father continued in a solemn voice, looking at each one of them. "With an arrogant king, we had no choice but to continue meeting in secret to interpret the Bible as we pleased."

Mary held her locket and thought, *Maybe this is what adversity means.*

"A wave of terror swept the countryside and we had to be close-mouthed as we made concealed plans to leave England. We dearly loved our country, but we feared for our lives so we gathered ye up with only the belongings we could carry." At that, Mother rubbed her arms and tugged her sleeves down for warmth; although the fire was blazing on the hearth, it was as if a chill had settled in Mary's heart.

"That's true," father said, nodding his head.

Mary and her sisters wanted to know all of it but weren't certain that they could bear the realization of what they were hearing. Mary peeked at her sisters. Isabella sat still, struggling to hold back tears. Engle wasn't as teary eyed, but Mary remembered a day the previous year when Engle had told her something about those fearful days. The two of them had been walking along one of the many dikes that held the seawaters back from the low farmland. "No matter how terrible the consequence," Engle had told her, "our family was determined to be steadfast in our faith." Mary had felt a

---

[15] **Asylum**: place of safety

strange exultation hum through her at her sister's words. How proud she was for her family's courage. Waiting to hear more, the girls glanced at their father as he continued to tell them more of their trials from their past.

"King James did not approve of his subjects leaving England to find homes in other lands. William Brewster, the leading citizen among us, assured everyone that Holland was a beautiful, safe country where we could practice our religion."

Under her breath Mary asked quietly, "Was England beautiful?"

Mother overheard and responded, "Aye, I miss the misty mornings that faded as the cool wind blew through the vast fields . . . where thousands of yellow daffodils nodded in the afternoon sunshine."

In her family's faces, Mary could see the strain of haunting memories, but she was glad that they could hold on to little glimmers of happy memories that they could share tonight.

"Daughters, you were so young then and did not understand. Ye would ask, 'Why, why do we have to leave?' We wanted ye to grow up where we would be free to pray and live." Those powerful words stayed with the family.

Father stoked the fire and stirred up the embers to eliminate the chill in the air as Mary leaned up to her mother, who invited her to cuddle and get warm. She sank into her mother's arms, sharing her heavy knit shawl.

"We knew the escape would be dangerous during the day." Father's face was troubled. "We fled with only cloak and shawl through the darkest hours of the night. We went in haste and had to be absolutely silent, abandoning everything!"

Mum was nodding her head in agreement. "We moved hurriedly past dovecote granaries, bake houses, and the blacksmith's shop. I can see ye still, Mary, with your tear-stained cheeks, saying in your wee voice, 'Where will we sleep tonight?' I lifted ye up in my arms to move out faster. We were faced with heartbreaking choices, leaving everything that was familiar—our beloved village, our cottage, our furniture, our personal possessions, and, of course, some of our kind friends."

The girls were so absorbed listening that not one of them noticed Master Albert up on top of the table playing with the delicate threads that dangled from the workbaskets. Engle's cry frightened the cat, who leaped from the table, upsetting all the spools that fell from the baskets. With threads caught in his paw, Master Albert unraveled hours of intricate lace as he dashed about, winding threads around the leg of the table and across the floor! Hollering and in tears, Engle chased after Mary's naughty cat and shot accusing glances at her little sister.

Mary felt sorry for Master Albert. He was just being curious and didn't mean any harm, yet she felt responsible for the awful mess that had her sister crying. With all of the confusion and excitement, it was difficult to settle everyone down. Master Albert was captured and scolded soundly, and Isabella tried to comfort Engle as Father's calming voice called everyone to prayer.

The fire faded and so did the evening. Prayer began their day and closed each night. "Daughters, all is forgiven. It is getting late and ye must have your rest." With a resolute voice, their father began to pray. After his solemn prayer, he spoke again in the stillness of the room. "Always remember, freedom of religion for all men involves suffering, hardship, and sacrifice.[16] Afraid to do

---

[16] **Sacrifice:** to give up something

something, but doing it anyway, that's what makes us strong." Mary's head was spinning, not just from the late hour, but with the many emotions this evening of tales had awakened. With candlestick in hand, Mary made her way to bed.

Mary wanted to be strong, but she could feel her heart pounding. Sadness and fear had been a large part of her family's life. Even though it left a sick feeling in her stomach to hear what had happened, she wanted to know every last detail. This was her story too. She lay still in her bed, bunching the coverlet up under her chin, and frightening thoughts raced through her head. If they could be forced to leave England in order to find freedom to follow their faith in peace, could the same thing happen in Amsterdam?

She was grateful when Mother came over and sat next to her on the bed. "Mother, when we wake up on the morrow, will we still be together and safe?" Mary pulled her mother in close and inhaled the familiar rosewater scent from her mother's warm skin and a hint of lavender from her clothes. "Don't go! Stay with me a bit more," she whispered. "I know I'm supposed to be English, but I still feel like a Dutch girl."

Mary's mother stroked her hair reassuringly. "Ye were born in England . . . that makes you one hundred percent an English girl."

Master Albert came out from hiding and gingerly leaped up onto the foot of the bed, spreading himself out and warming Mary's feet.

"We are safe and sound here in Holland, Mary. Ye need not worry. The Dutch people are kind to us." Mother began to sing a song to soothe her.

It seems so far and yet so near.
I hear a distant song, it fills the air.

I know the time will come, a day of freedom.
The land I hope where there is no more fear.
I see another time another place.

"Mum, please tuck me in."

Her mother moved the coverlet under her softly yet snugly enough to keep in the warmth, bundling Mary into her cubbyhole bed hidden in the wall behind curtains and said, "Ye needn't fret. I give thee good night. Now be merry in your heart."

Her mother's calmness filled Mary with peace, and she slipped into a sound sleep with Master Albert purring his usual steady purr.

Chapter 3
Many Miles

MASTER ALBERT'S PERSISTENT RESTLESSNESS and mewing made Mary's father curious.

"Mary, is your cat trying to tell us something? He keeps on pacing back and forth in front of the hearth?"

"He is just cold and wants to be warm," she answered.

But Father thought otherwise. "No, there's something else. After three days of sudden rain squall and downpour, the fearsome wind last night hurled currents of air that filled our chimney with debris. Perhaps the grid on top needs cleaning and adjusting?"

After Master Chilton cleared away the rubble and waste, he studied the pitch of the roof and the ridge. Back on the ground, he announced that their chimney was clear and safe to continue fires in their hearth. The neighbors, however, feared that storks, winging their way along with the north wind, would soon find and expect many nesting places on their roofs, and especially in their chimney tops.

"Ahh," Father said with a smile, "so that's what Master Albert was hoping for, Mary. He's waiting for a nice plump stork to come down our chimney!"

The winter nights were long, and Mary's family, bone cold, clustered close to each other around the fire. Master Albert was now back in good graces and accepted as "keeper of the hearth" and earned his keep by the amount of mice, and even a few rats, he captured.

Father had just finished reading to them from the Bible and said with conviction, "I believe we all have been created for greater things than we can even comprehend. Hard times call for great things—things in the noblest and redemptive sense are predicated upon tolerance, love, respect, understanding, dignity, prayer, and God."

He then took notice that Mary's mind seemed to be far away. "Daughter, is everything well with ye?"

Mary nodded slowly, wanting to share a wish with her father, but not sure how to ask. Engle spoke up softly. "Father, may I speak?"

"Aye," he said firmly raising one brow.

"Mary wants to hear about that night in England when our family walked."

"Truly, Mary?" he asked.

This time Mary nodded quickly and sat up with her legs crossed.

"Mother and I are fearful of telling you daughters too much of our heartache."

Now mother spoke, trying hard to keep her voice steady and calm. "We must have walked at least ten leagues. That's over twenty-five miles! Some families tried to flee on ships and were caught by harbor authorities. Other Scrooby Separatists who were our friends were imprisoned. After several failed attempts, many families decided to slip away a few at a time, rather than attempt to escape in a single large group. We chose to keep our family together, come what may. The first night with no moon, it was dark and difficult to find our way, and with English authorities watching at every port, we had to be extremely careful not to get caught and be forced to surrender."

"We walked most of the way in darkness. It was necessary to do so—it was safer to keep moving and travel by night. At times we traveled over frost-covered farmland with no sign of human habitation anywhere in sight. Then, one late winter night, thankfully a sliver of a moon appeared and guided us to the next nearest barn and shack, where we found a place to lay our heads and hide in the hay. Each night, Mary, you lay completely quiet and covered, hidden with us, not making a single sound nor ring."

Mary loved the sound of her mother's calm voice and was engrossed in every word. Still, it felt strange to know she had been part of the adventure mother was telling. Try as she might, she couldn't bring any clear memories to mind, just a blur of shadows crossing the stage of her mind. She moved to be near her mother and felt a certain closeness as her mother carried on.

"For a long time we had been trying to secure passage on a ship from England to Holland. We gave two shillings for permission to board a prearranged boat waiting in the darkest hour of the night in a silent harbor, trusting that the crew would not expose us to the authorities but take us safely across the water. It was this last critical hour that was most terrifying."

Father added, "The night was so dark we were not able to see in front of our noses. We left from the mouth of the River Stour heading toward the North Sea and on to Holland. We dared to hardly breathe for fear we would get caught."

"We remained still as the boat moved through a strange new sea. From the rush and swirl of water, we began to feel seasick. After a long while we could see that the scenery was changing. 'Twas hard to identify at first, with lots of pathways and wide water canals. Our sailor, without a word, held firm to the oar. Large windmills seemed to rise straight from the ocean, for the land was so flat that it was lower than the ocean. Long dikes had been built to keep the seawater out, and the windmills pumped the water away from the land. In the faint starlight, they loomed high in the sky.

This would be our new home, where we would speak a different language and learn new ways, not knowing what lay ahead for any of us. We came with very little means, not a penny in our pockets, arriving close to where we are living right now, near the harbor, here in Amsterdam. One thing kept us going. We knew that we were one family sharing an inheritance of faith."

Mary thought about her mother's words. An inheritance was a gift, passed on from parents to children. At that moment, Mary wouldn't have traded her family's inheritance for gold or silver. Without being told, she knew how rich they were to be able to pray together. She couldn't imagine not being able to hear her father read from the Bible as the family gathered together in love at the end of each day. She was glad her parents had been brave enough to leave England. And then, with her head full of stories and her heart full of love for her family, she fell asleep where she leaned against her mother's shoulder.

Chapter 4
Klompen Shoes

AFTER A FEW MORE NIGHTS around the hearth, Mother thought it sound to tell cheerful stories for a change.

"Mary dear, because ye were the youngest, ye fared well. Ye and the Brewster's little daughter, Fear, who was a bit younger than ye, were good chums. Soon after we arrived, the two of ye skipped along the footpath holding hands, up over a bridge, until you came to an open field filled with a thousand colorful flowers. Both of ye returned to  our little alley home with fists full of colorful tulips. Ye made new friends immediately. Even though life is hard here in Amsterdam, ye and your little companions have had no trepidation."[17]

Father smiled and said, "Aye, as night drew near, Mary, ye would change into nightclothes and climb into your hideaway bed built into the wall. The new language was difficult for mother and me, but because ye were so young, ye learned the new words quickly,

---

[17] **Trepidation**: fear, worry

better than anyone else in the family. Every night we could hear thee reciting Dutch words into the still of night."

"Bijbel"	Bible
"Goede Morgen"	Good morning
"Behagen"	Please
"Dank U usel"	Thank you very much
"Vergiffenis"	Pardon
"Goede dag"	Good-bye
"Muts"	Bonnet

Mary's face lit up and she giggled as Father spoke the Dutch words with his English accent.

"Mary, ye would repeat the words and phrases over and over again until ye began to sound like an authentic Dutch girl."

"Dutch attire was strange to us," Mother continued, "but we liked the pretty lace collars, and the Dutch coif[18] that covers our hair, and the big "klompen," the wooden shoes that keep our feet dry. Daughters, ye learned properly how to wear the winged caps on your heads. Now you sturdily braid each other's hair, brushing out the snarls, and use colorful ribbon artfully woven to go around the bun at the back of your heads."

"A lot of frippery,"[19] Father added, turning his head with his eyebrow raised. "'Tis folly!"

The older girls enjoyed all the extra frills but could see that their father had heard enough idle talk.

"'Tis late in the night. Let us kneel for family prayer and haste to our resting place."

After another long day, they took up their candles and all went

---

[18] **Coif:** a head covering for girls and women made of white linen

[19] **Frippery:** showy display in dress

off to bed dutifully. Engle drew the dark curtains near their bedside and blew out the candle.

In the Chilton home, as in everyone's home at the time, clothes were used as long as they could be repaired. Laundry was only done, by hand, four to five times a year. And they had just two meals a day and only fathers and mothers could sit down at mealtime. The children always had to stand at the table. Everyone ate with their fingers and knives. That was just how things were done those

hundreds of years ago. The kitchen was always the warmest, busiest room, as the hearth glowed all day long and through many frigid nights.

Goodwife Chilton thrust the poker in the fire to adjust the coals, then filled the pot of boiling water with fresh vegetables and herbs. Isabella depended on the firelight to sew and mend, while Engle and Mary warmed their cold stocking feet, and Father stacked the chopped wood and filled the bucket with

lumps of coal. Their lives centered on each other and the reassuring warmth of their affection.

As the sun set the next evening, Mary hugged her cloak around herself and hunched her shoulders against the cold wind. She knew her mother expected her to be home long before now—she had simply lost track of time. Late in the afternoon, when she had finished cleaning the dishes from the midday meal and hanging out the bed linens to dry in the fresh air and sunshine, she decided to do the same. With her afternoon tasks finished, she had tucked a crust of rye bread and a sliver of hard cheese into her apron pocket and was soon traveling her favorite walking path. Mary loved this time of day, when the sun traded places with the moon and the evening air was crisp and sweet. When the sun finally slipped below the horizon, she turned for home. Her older sisters were helping with the evening meal when she burst through the door.

They looked up with worry and disapproval. Isabella asked with disfavor, "Where have ye been?"

"Thou art late." Father gave a stern, admonishing look.

Pulling her hood off her hair, Mary said, "I beg your pardon, Father. I didn't realize the lateness of the hour." She knew she should have paid closer attention to the time. This was once too often that she had alarmed her family.

"Oh, my! Child, ye are sopping." Her mother shook her head.

She was not the kind to reproach, but she took one look at Mary's muddy, soggy skirts, and Mary knew what Mother was thinking—surely she would be confined and masked by chills.

"Toast thyself at the fire." Mother bade her remove her wet cloak and damp woolen stockings.

Supper was usually a most cheerful meal with light laughter, but this evening there was no laughter at all. Mary tried not to notice her family's grim reaction. She found her proper place at the table and stood next to Isabella, who gave her a push in the small of her back. She folded her skinny arms.

Master Albert pried himself from the cushions in the chair, stretched, and then jumped lightly across the floor to rub up against Mary's cold legs, purring as if to say, "I'm glad you're home."

Like her mother, her sisters were well-groomed, dressed in fleecy wool with white linen collars and aprons. Mother's frock[20]

---

[20] **Frock**: a dress

was a dark gray and her sisters' were the color of blueberries in the summer. Mary felt scraggly among them.

Everyone bowed their heads as Father gave a proper blessing on the food. Feeling a blush spread across her cheeks, she shivered a bit and shifted her weight from foot to foot, trying to get warm and find a comfortable position. As always, her parents sat at each end of the table while the three girls remained standing. Chilled and tired, Mary longed to sit down by the fire, but she picked up her small bowl, sipping the hot potato soup made with barley, onions, and warm, creamy milk.

Many months passed, and one evening Father brought the family around the hearth to tell them that they would soon leave Amsterdam to settle in a place called Leyden.

Mother said, "I thought it would come to this all along—the city is too dark, dirty, and noisy. Leyden will be much like the countryside that we dearly loved in England."

Both Father and Mother felt it best to leave the sophisticated city and its worldly influence and, along with many of their congregation, move away. Neither Mary nor her sisters said a word. Mary couldn't remember England. This was the only home she knew. She liked the hustle and bustle of the city around them. And her comfortable bed nook. And what about her friends? What if she would never see them again?

Mum broke the silence, adding softly, "Father will have tailor work there, and we women will have plenty to keep our hands busy."

Most of the men had provided for their families as simple farmers in England, but in this new land they found few jobs open to them because they were not citizens of Holland. Moving to the countryside, the farmers could begin farming again, and it would help their children to better remember Scrooby, Sherwood Forest, and Canterbury, England.

"In Leyden," their mother told them, "you will still be able to ice skate on the canals in the winter and pick tulips in the spring, and with the Dutch side by side, we'll still participate in Meerderheid[21] and together sweep the streets clean."

Father quickly added, "And your friends and their families will be coming too."

This made Mary feel much better, until she thought of a new fear. "Will Master Albert have to stay behind?"

"Well, we can't have that. Of course he will come!" Father answered with a snappy wink. "There will be plenty of mice in Leyden!"

"Oh, thank ye, Father!"

---

[21] **Meerderheid:** a festival when Dutch people clean their streets

Chapter 5
Inside a Windmill

MOST OF THE FAMILIES in their congregation found places to live in the poorest section of Leyden, down an alley called Stunksteeg—Stink Alley, which they quickly renamed Choir Alley. It made them feel better about themselves, but changing the name didn't change their meager surroundings. Master Bradford found lodging with the Brewster family near where he had his printing press. The Chilton family found a more acceptable home in a windmill in the countryside just outside of Leyden. It stood near a canal in a little village called Green Gate, where others of their congregation had settled. Mary loved her new home from the start. To others, it may have seemed humble, but Mary felt like she was living inside a castle. She would lean out one of the high windows above and wave to her friends.

"Hello down there!"

Life was slower in Green Gate, and the people were hard working. The first morning in their new home, the sun had risen well above the horizon like a slash of gold.

"Here we need not lock our doors, and we can have a kitchen garden just outside our door to grow herbs, vegetables, and gully flowers and primroses!"

Mary's mother was happy to have a garden profuse with wild beans shooting up, a corner set aside for a pig, and a rooster crowing on the gatepost. An old discarded wooden shoe on the kitchen stoop was used for Master Albert's warm milk and daily leftovers.

The white-washed lime walls gleamed in the sun, and flower boxes bloomed at each small window.

Mum happily said, "Flowers mean you are here to stay."

The inside of the windmill looked twice as high as Mary looked down at the oaken doorway below. A groan and squeak came from the constant churning of the mill. For this reason, the Chiltons didn't have to pay quite the amount as others did for their housing. The family always left their wooden shoes outside on the doorsteps. From Mary's view out the second-story window, they looked like doll shoes, and the pig looked tiny and far away, and Leyden town seemed miniature.

Moving to Leyden was not the only big change for Mary's family. Soon after their move, Isabella met a young weaver named Richard. Before long, he was sharing evening meals with the family and taking walks with Isabella with Mary trailing along behind as chaperone. One day he came to visit Father, and after a long talk, an announcement was made. Isabella would marry Richard, but though she would live only a few streets away and see her family every day, Mary felt a little sad. She would miss Isabella's teasing and even her bossiness, but that was the way of things. Someday Engle would also get married, and then Mary's turn would come. But that day was still far away.

Green Gate was a safe and happy community until the day Mary and her new friend Abigail were on their way home, walking cheerfully along as their wooden shoes clattered along the icy, cobblestone footpath. The cold air swirled around them, and they could see their breath as they puffed on their hands. Suddenly Mary heard a frightful call.

"Mary, Mary, come quick!"

Dirk and Deliverance, two of her friends, came running to her, "It's your father, Mary. Your father has been hurt! Some hoodlums beat him—it's dreadful!"

A wave of fear washed over Mary. Her legs felt frozen, but somehow she found the will to move and ran the rest of the way home, followed by her friends. When she arrived at her father's side, she couldn't believe what she saw. His ankle was twisted, and his knee was injured, his blood seeping through his trousers. But the worst was the livid cut on his forehead. A surgeon had been sent for. In the meantime, Mother seemed to know just what to do and how to make him more comfortable.

At the sight of it all, Mary could not hold back her tears. He looked so pale. Why had this awful thing happened to her father? One by one, her friends gave her comfort.

Isabella recounted how she and Father had been on their way home from the textile market when they had been caught in the middle of a riot between two rival religious groups. A group of angry boys had thrown rocks, and one of them had hit Father in the head. Another had hit Isabella in the arm. She was bruised but had escaped the worst of it. Fortunate they were that some of their neighbors had been close by when the fighting started and were able to carry Father home.

The surgeon arrived, and after examining Father carefully,

concluded that the rock that had struck him had not broken his skull. With plenty of rest, he would recover. Mother was left to bandage Father up. Mary, along with her sisters and friends, sat silent and heartsick throughout the visit.

"It will take a few days and he will feel sluggish and low for a while, but your father will get better," Mary's mother said.

Her mother's hushed tones took the fear out of her heart. Still, Mary felt baffled and full of despair. Fear and sadness came to her thoughts as she looked again at her father's wounds.

How could such a thing happen to Father, who meant everything to her?

It was a painful lesson: life could change with every breath taken. But it came hand in hand with the gift of love: all of their close neighbors reached out to the Chilton family with goodwill, supporting them through this difficult time.

Chapter 6
Remy and Prudence

GREEN GATE POPULATION DOUBLED every Thursday as venders gathered with newly cut tulips, produce, and baked goods. The villagers carried fresh milk in jugs and fish from the sea to the market. Ravenous caws came from the harbor gulls, scavenging among the stalls. The clanking of wooden carts pulled by vendors with their faint shouting rolled up and down the rutted main road that lay outside their front door.

Helping on market day was Mary's favorite chore. Isabella was the one entrusted with a few meager coins, which had to be carefully budgeted for the week's supplies. But Mary carried a large woven basket with which to bring home their purchases. Usually they ate simple fare—turnips, potatoes, peas and lentils, even onions and

barley, cooked into soups. But today they had a special treat: a wheel of golden yellow Edam cheese, covered in bright red wax. Mary's mouth was already watering at the thought of the nutty, buttery cheese.

After stopping at the last booth, Mary hurried ahead of her sister, eager to get home to the windmill house. "Mum, are ye there?"

Through the open top half of the Dutch door, she turned the metal latch and paused to look back over her shoulder at the flat wet meadowlands and farther across the canals to the level fields where she could see the sharp roof lines and hay stacks.

The sound of her voice echoed off the walls. Master Albert came running to meet her, his fluffy tail rubbing against her leg.

"What a faithful cat ye are!"

Every afternoon he was always waiting in the little window for her to return. Mary scooped him up and nuzzled his soft head with her chin.

"Did ye have a pleasant day playing with some mice? Did ye?" she murmured. Master Albert's rumbly purring filled Mary with happiness. What a dear little chum he was.

Supper was a feast with the addition of the cheese, and everyone went to bed with full stomachs and pleasantly satisfied.

That night while lying in bed, Mary heard her mother say, "Husband, dear, Leyden is a beautiful town built on small islands joined by fine bridges, but little Green Gate, oh, I feel that I could live here forever."

Mary loved their newfound home and Green Gate, which was a quaint village with a central open market in the middle. Just behind the market, the steeple of Pieterskerk towered over all the other rooftops. Small houses nestled in a line with large windmills behind. Mary thought their windmill was a perfect medium size, just right for their comfort and nearest in the direction of the village. Farther down the lane in the other direction was Green Close, a peaceful, large house where they worshipped.

The sky loomed a bright, endless blue under the blinding white sun, perfect for a new field of sprouting tulips. In her alcove at the upper far end of the room, draped in hand-spun linen cloth, Mary lay in bed thinking about the beauty of their home. She fell asleep listening to the groan and squeaking sound of the large arms reaching out with the endless turning of the windmill that by now had become a soothing tone.

Neeltje, Humility, and Prudence were a few of Mary's new friends. Then there was Remy, a Dutch boy who liked to draw pictures. He was especially fond of Mary.

"Remy is short for Rembrandt," she told her mother. "He was born here in Leyden and speaks Dutch the best I've heard. Neeltje told me that he likes to draw and paint paintings with a brush. But on market days he helps unload the day's catch of slippery, shimmering herring still flopping in their containers. He told me I could come and watch him empty the fish if I wanted to."

Everyone wanted to be Mary's friend. She was good-natured, kind, and made a fun game out of most everything. She was always eager to join in with whatever experience would come next. Remy showed them how to make toy pinwheels. They were like small windmills pinned to a stick that would twirl in the wind as the children ran.

Even though the harbor was some distance from Mary's windmill, she could faintly hear the morning boats preparing to leave for the day's fishing, with fisherman calling to one another and gulls crying. From her windmill house the winds would carry the oily, salty scent of herring, which always lingered in the air.

In Leyden, water-filled canals and dikes held back the sea from flooding the land. The huge windmills continued to pump and splash. From the sea, raw gusts of salty wind whipped up a spray that leaped the dike. But now the air was fresh again.

"Mind your step!" Mary called out excitedly to Remy and Prudence as they skipped along holding their new pinwheels high in the air, following behind her on the windswept dike. "Let's all go and sit on the wall of the dike," Mary suggested.

Remy and Prudence agreed, and soon they sat dangling their feet, watching a slow boat come pushing around a bend in the canal. The oarsmen on deck waved to them as they lowered the sails so the boat could glide under the low footbridge.

Mary jumped up. "I have an idea. Let's run along and follow the boat. Come quick before it gets away!"

She looked up at the seagulls swirling and sailing far out to sea. She enjoyed the freedom of running along the windswept embankment and wondered to herself what it would be like to fly and be as free as one of those birds. How did those little creatures so far up in the sky and away from the earth know where they were going?

More and more, like many of her friends, Mary was expected to weave, to become an "Yperlinge" alongside the other women and work long hours in the mills. As the season turned from summer to winter to spring, the hay meadows turned green again after their first cut. The sheep had grown white and fluffy with new wool. As Mary washed the dirty wool clipped from the sheep, she found it hard to pay attention as all her thoughts wandered to the sun-filled meadows and the bustle of the harbor. But her pleasant daydreams were interrupted by Engle's sharp complaints.

"Mary, I'm losing patience with thee. I cannot comb or spin this wet wool! The clippings are yet too dirty. Please try to give more heart to your task."

"I feel sorry for the sheep with no coats to keep them warm," Mary said sadly.

"Keep a mind on your work, Mary," Engle insisted.

Instead, Mary thought of poor Albert, alone in the windmill house . . . and his coat of fur. What if someone sheered it all off? How would that be? What would he do to keep warm? Life just didn't seem fair sometimes. Not for her father, set upon by ruffians in the street. Not for her friends and family, driven out of England simply over their faith and convictions. Not even for a simple creature like Master Albert. Was life meant to be this difficult?

Their mother, with her aching back, sat in the dimly lit mill with the other women and wove the thread into a fine linen cloth. Even with all the hours spent working, the families could not begin to earn enough money.

With the fishing fleet long since out of sight and far beyond the dike, Remy was now finished with his work for the day and on his way home. He caught up with Mary as she was returning from working in the mill.

He picked a blue cornflower out of the fields and ran up beside her. Catching his breath, he handed her the flower. "Here, for you!"

"Remy, thank ye." She cast a brief look at his smelly clothes, "What were your tasks today?"

"Oh, I helped at the marketplace when the fishing fleet arrived. Pardon the odor. I sorted and cleaned fish. I don't mind hard work, but I tire of it and long to . . ." He paused. "I long to do something else, not just wash off fish."

Mary got a whiff of the fishy smell and responded with a wrinkled nose and a laugh. She stuck the flower behind her ear inside her coif and said, "You could come and work with all of us in the woolen mill."

She turned, leading the way along a narrow, meandering lane, heading toward the outskirts of the village and to the open fields. Only now, farther on down the footpath, did Mary realize how cold the breeze off the sea was.

As they strolled along, she asked, "Remy, if ye had a chance to do anything else, anything at all, what would you like to do?"

He picked up a smooth rock and skipped it into the canal. "Someday I want to seriously paint."

His face was radiant. "As long as I can remember, I've loved to draw things. People tell me 'tis a waste of effort."

Mary had heard tittle-tattle that he was talented in such a way, but this was the first time he had opened up and shared his feelings with her. Remy watched her intently, as if to see whether she would agree or laugh, but Mary was listening earnestly.

"I've hardly told anyone about my dream to draw and paint before. Shapes, designs, and profusion of the deepest rich colors captivate me."

Mary wanted to respond, but at that moment, her eyes watered with the glaze of the sun and she began to blink.

"Mary, what is it? Is something in your eye?"

If she was honest with herself, it wasn't just the sun. Remy's dream had spoken to her heart. Caught off guard by the feelings stirring in her, she made a show of wiping her eyes with her apron. "Aye, the mill is dark inside. I hadn't realized this to be a most lovely day."

Her body ached, her skin itched as though she were wrapped tight in wool and could not stretch—it felt so good to her to be out in the fresh air. Remy was very observant and looked at her delicate, beautiful features, pale as porcelain,[22] with a smattering of tiny freckles across the bridge of her nose.

"Your cheeks are a beautiful pink." He smiled, and she laughed a little shyly at the compliment, bumping him with her shoulder.

As they walked along, her skirts fluttered in the wind. "Remy, why don't ye paint? Ye could give the world more unique beauty, something that no one else has done."

Mary and Remy exchanged looks. Now it was Remy's turn to be bashful. After a moment, he changed the subject.

"Look at you, Mary . . . you have a perfect smile."

Self-conscious, she pressed her lips together, trying not to smile.

"See? There it is, and now you are blushing."

Mary stole a glance at him. She wanted to say something but at that moment they both broke into laughter.

"I'll race you up to that field of flowers," he challenged.

Mary rolled her eyes. "I'd like to see ye try," she said in a teasing challenge as she took off running and laughing. He let her get ahead of him, then ran up behind her and caught her by her sash.

"Mary, Mary, I almost let you get away!"

Laughing and out of breath, they took hold of each other's hands and walked together the rest of the way to her home.

That night, Mary listened to her father's whispering voice through the large windmill house as it echoed softly from her parents' bedchamber and off the surface of the towering walls.

---

[22] **Porcelain:** translucent ceramic or china

"Goodwife," he said, "maybe one day I could have a tailor shop again like I had in England? After all, everyone must have clothes to wear. In the New World there could be homes and farms, and we could have our own church."

Her mother responded quietly, "Aye, husband, and raise our children and grandchildren to love and serve God. But my dear, Leyden is thousands of miles from such a dream as this New World."

"Aye, it's true, my Goodwife, but if we are open to it—the smallest miracle can change our lives."

Mary leaned against the wall and strained to pick every word out of the quiet conversation. Her own name spoken in a whisper caught her attention. She knew her parents were concerned, by the tone of their voices.

". . . no real future exists for the Pilgrims in Holland!" her mother said.

"No one really knows how far it will be by ship," her father replied firmly. "But I do not want my children to continue working long hours. I want them to keep their English customs and language and marry their own English people."

Mary turned her head on her pillow and stared through the partly opened curtains of the little window into the dim April night. For many days and weeks, she had caught snippets of similar conversations. While the adults tried to keep their words away from young ears, Mary had pieced enough together to know exactly what was going on. They were talking about leaving their adopted land and setting out on a dangerous journey to the New World. A shiver scurried down Mary's back, but she couldn't say if it was from fear or excitement. To set sail across the immense ocean in search of a new home seemed the stuff of stories or dreams. Down at the harbor with Remy, she had often watched the great sailing ships disappearing over the horizon. She had never imagined that she might one day take passage on one of them. She snuggled more deeply into her featherbed, her mind filled with great white sails and strange shores. During the night there was the slightest veering of the north wind, so slight it could be noticed only by a windmill, as Mary was lulled to sleep.

Chapter 7
Mary's Anguish

SEVERAL DAYS LATER IN the center of the settlement, a large group gathered around to consider Mary's father as he spoke.

"All great and honorable actions are accompanied with great difficulties," he announced to their congregation.

Paying close heed from behind, Mary stood silently watching and listening as she nibbled a ragged fingernail. She was anxious to finally hear all the rumors and speculation that had been traded behind closed doors and late at night.

He continued, ". . . for each new generation needs to be stronger than the last."

Mary tried to blend in with the crowd that had gathered around to listen.

". . . creating a colony in the New World is an ambitious venture. All manner of adversity and hardship will be our constant companions."

There was that word again. *Adversity.* It pricked Mary's ears, and she listened more intently to what her father was saying to the villagers. They were a poor but a respected group who continued to talk about an eventual departure.

She heard, "There are two hundred by now." Two hundred people willing to make the dangerous journey to the New World?

Mary was fearful and fascinated at the same time. She knew her father longed to find a country where they would have peace and freedom, but the New World seemed impossibly far away.

The congregational members managed to make a living and support their church, but now, everyone was gossiping about the rampant rumors of a war brewing between Holland and Spain. The Chilton family, along with many of their friends and neighbors, longed for a peaceful place. The time had come to make the important move.

Mary slipped into a daydream and didn't hear another word Father was saying. She was totally absorbed in imagining the new life that might be waiting for them in a New World. Mary caught her father's eye. A look of concern clouded his expression, and she reached up and touched her treasured locket, seeking reassurance.

Many of the older folks in town were making serious plans to sail. Tears suddenly filled Mary's eyes at the realization that their lives were changing again, at the serious decisions being made. How could she ever bear to leave her friends? Mary thought about the inscription on her locket nestled safely around her neck. "Sweet are the uses of adversity." She wasn't really sure what adversity meant, but as she repeated the words again to herself, they gave her a strange kind of comfort as she thought of how she might have to leave and say good-bye to all her friends.

Holland had been her home for almost ten years. The few memories she had of England were like dreams that started to fade upon waking. Ten years was far too short a time to spend with dear friends and in a beloved country. But in the end, the merry little band of English Separatists and Dutch children who had grown up together would say a sad farewell to each other.

Every family worked frantically to get needed provisions. There were kettles, pewter,[23] dishes, skillets, bellows,[24] cups, jugs, tubs, bedding, and linens. There were special things needed for small children and babies too.

Fathers needed every size and variety of saws, axes, hatchets, grindstones[25] and anvils.[26] They would need giant screws to put up a church, houses, and sheds. Lines and hooks for fishing, and pistols, swords, powder, and muskets[27] for protection were on the list. Everyone had two proper questions that must be asked as they decided what to pack and what to leave: "Has this served its purpose?" and "Do I have room to carry and manage this?"

"We ought to make plans about how we are going to be prepared," Mother said. "We are departing in a fortnight."[28] Mary made a face and shook her head at the thought.

"Come, Mary, that's enough of that, child! Father needs our help, and we need to get on with it. Now keep your chin up," she said impatiently. "Be of good cheer."

Mary managed to smile a little, though her face was drawn with pain as she bit her lower lip, and her smile soon faded.

"Mary, I can see that ye have a heavy heart." Her mother pulled her closer. "Ye know strength isn't something we have. It's something God helps us find. We usually find it a day at a time."

"Being strong can be a very lonely thing," Mary said under her breath.

"Come and help me with some of the items we need to check off."

---

[23] **Pewter:** made from an alloy of tin with lead, bronze, or copper

[24] **Bellows:** used for blowing fires

[25] **Grindstone:** a revolving stone disk for sharpening most tools or polishing things

[26] **Anvil:** an iron or steel block on which metal objects are hammered into shapes

[27] **Musket:** a type of gun

[28] **Fortnight:** two weeks

As Mary sorted through a chest, dividing items into "pack" or "leave" piles, her mother said, "Mary, there is something that we need to talk about." Mary looked up at her mother's serious tone.

"Now, I want ye to be brave. We need to decide together as to who will give a proper home to Master Albert."

"What? Leave Master Albert?!" Mary's heart froze. Saying good-bye to friends and home had been hard enough, but she could bear it because of her pet. The thought of leaving him behind broke her heart. She fell to the floor.

"I can't leave him, I can't," she pleaded on her knees. "Please Mum, don't make me say good-bye to him too!"

"It is not prudent, Mary, to bring a cat with us. I know how ye feel . . ."

"No, no, ye don't know how much I love Albert!"

"Come, come, now. We are all making sacrifices for the better good. Who do ye think would give him the most suitable care?" Her mother rubbed her back, and her voice sounded suspiciously shaky. Mary thought if she were to look up, she would see tears in her mother's eyes as well. Mother continued, "Sit up and dry your eyes and try to understand. We must put our shoulders to the wheel."

Mary couldn't answer, she was so choked with tears. It was just too much for her to give up her little chum, Albert.

Clothes were made in dark colors. On the Sabbath and for funerals they wore blacks and grays, and for everyday they wore dark blues, russet browns, and forest greens. This was common among the English lower classes from which they sprang. Mary's mother measured her for clothing to be worn for at least a year.

"What color do ye like the most, Mary?" her mother asked.

Mary didn't have to think twice. "Red. I wish to have a red

frock the color of holly berries to wear aboard the ship so when I depart and wave good-bye, my friends will be sure to see me from a long ways away . . ."

"Oh, Mum." She broke into sobs, the tears streaming down her young face. "I can't bear to go so far away to an unknown world beyond the vast ocean."

"Mary, dear, ye'll make new friends, I promise ye—and keep your old friends too." Her mother tried to help her be stouthearted as she used a remnant piece of linen to wipe her tears.

The next thing Mary knew, her mother had stitched a fresh new frock and linen coif for her.

"Thank thee, Mum. It suits me very well."

"Indeed, sweetheart," her mother said, reaching out with her arms to give her a hug. "'Tis a tender time for us, but we are made of stern stuff."

Mary's mother and sisters had worked from daylight until dark making ready the food and clothing, for it was no slight task to prepare for such a long journey. Her mother carefully packed only the items they would need: a pewter pitcher, iron pot, brass kettle, and so forth.

"We are now properly packed and finished at last, without loss of temper!" Mary saw tears in her mother's eyes as she took a deep breath and put her hand on her chest. "Be still my heart."

"Mum, what's wrong?" Mary asked.

"Oh, Mary dear, only ye and I and your father will be going."

In disbelief, Mary put her hand over her mouth.

"Your older sister Isabella is staying behind with her husband and children, and Engle will stay and continue to work in the mill."

"Mum," Mary could hardly speak, "they are our family. How can we leave them here? I will sorely miss them."

Wiping her tears and Mary's too with her skirt, her mother said with new courage, "We hope they will join us in a few years."

Mary had a mixture of feelings now that her sisters would not be coming. How could she begin to be happy about such a change in her life? She was excited to sail on a ship, yet at the same time forlorn—what fun could it be without Albert, her sisters and her good friends, as well as Remy?

"A huge ship!" Mary tried to be excited while telling her friends. She wondered to herself if they could be happy about such news. "The leaders are going to buy a ship for our voyage."

"What kind of a ship? What voyage?" Remy asked.

Mary shook her head. "I don't know, but a man in London will give a lot of money if everyone will promise to work for seven years to pay him back."

Prudence spoke up. "My family has changed their minds about going."

Mary's heart sunk yet again. She had been counting on Prudence, her dear friend, to be on the voyage with her and in the New World. Why was her family just giving up?

"My father says it's too far and not a fair agreement."

Another friend added, "Me brother told me deep in the sea there are frightening sea serpents[29] and across the sea there are savage men that wear feathers all over them!"

A few of the girls winced and squealed.

Even though Mary had thought about these things day and night, she scrunched up her shoulders, put on a bright smile, and said, "I think it's going to be a fine adventure!" Yet her eyes said something else, and she was trying hard to convince herself to keep her chin up.

Within a few days, a gathering took place where Mary stood nearby as William Brewster, the Separatist leader, said, "We have

---

[29] **Serpent:** a snake

courage enough to face whatever may happen," and stepped forward to accept the agreement. So did Mary's father, the Bradford, Allerton, and Rogers families, as well as several others. Forty Separatists in all. Still, this was not enough from the Green Gate colony. So arrangements were made for additional families to join them on their journey.

"Strangers," as the Green Gate group called them, from London and Southern England would join the main party for departure in Southampton, England. The only ship they could afford was an old, battered ship leftover from England's war against the Spanish Armada. After many repairs and after new sails were added, the *Speedwell* was ready to sail to England. They would sail alongside a larger ship named the *Mayflower* to the New World.

Mary was aware of the conflicting feelings that hung over their group. Some of them were leaving and some of them were choosing to stay behind in Leyden. Sadness was visible on everyone's faces as they went about making their final preparations. It was apparent that thoughts of leaving dear ones and friends whom they would never see again, and thoughts of the terrible hardships that would be required on a long ocean voyage, were on everyone's minds.

The Chilton family joined the first wave of bold, brave Pilgrims to travel from Green Gate in Leyden to depart from Delft Haven and on to Southampton, England. Mary held on to Master Albert as long as she possibly could.

Isabella had agreed to take care of her cat, brush him, and feed him well. She promised Mary, "Ye needn't worry, sister dear. Albert will be loved and kept warm by our hearth."

It was a most dreaded and yet tender parting! Mary hugged the cat's neck and buried her face in his fur.

"Good-bye, me little chum . . ." Mary shook his soft, fuzzy paw. Warm tears rolled down her cheeks. "You've been a good kitty-cat,

Master Albert. I will miss ye!" Slowly, she placed him into the arms of her sister.

Tomorrow they would be leaving. Mary dreaded the day. On a grassy knoll along the windy dike, she threw her arms around her two dearest friends as they all stood in a huddle. They stood in silence, staring at the ground, unable to say a word. Heartbroken, they couldn't look each other in the eye.

Prudence, with tears brimming, was the first to break the silence. "Is not every end a new beginning? Ye will do well, Mary. One thing I know for sure, our friendship will never end."

They hugged each other tight as long, painful moments passed.

"When will I see ye again?" Mary cried. "Promise me ye'll come to the New World. With every ship that arrives, I'll look for ye."

With a lump in her throat, Mary swallowed hard and tried to calm her quivering voice. They all put their arms around each other one last time. They realized all too well what this farewell meant.

Now everyone was sobbing! Just as Mary turned to leave, Remy caught her by the hand to pull her back and said, "Wait!" He took something that was rolled up from inside his doublet[30] and gave it to Mary.

"Here is a little something I drew for ye. I hope ye like it."

Surprised at the unexpected gift, Mary excitedly unrolled the parchment[31] paper to see a lovely drawing of a windmill.

"Oh, Remy," she cried out, "my windmill castle!" Her eyes lit up. "It's beautiful! Ye drew our windmill house. Ye are the dearest lad I know! And look at me, my hands are empty. I wish I had a gift for ye."

He took her hand. "Your friendship, Mary, is gift enough. Be safe in the New World. Take courage, Mary!"

---

[30] **Doublet:** man's close-fitting jacket
[31] **Parchment:** the skin of a sheep or goat prepared for writing on.

Remy gave her a last embrace that lingered longer than before. The tears she thought she had under control started up again. Mary sobbed and turned reluctantly. She took a step from him, his hand still in hers until her next step broke their link. She didn't look back until she came to a bend in the path. Remy was still standing where she had left him. Waving her hand and tossing a kiss in the air, she at last turned and ran. Would she ever see him again?

That night, she slipped into her nightclothes and climbed into bed. Peeking out between the curtains, she had a good last view of the high walls made of hewn[32] tree trunks interwoven with branches and twigs inside their windmill house, cemented together with clay. A full moon peeked between two of the windmill arms. On her last night in the "windmill castle," Mary thought about her future on the other side of the earth without her sisters and friends, without her dear Master Albert. During the night she tossed and turned and dreamed hazy images of a wondrous journey ahead.

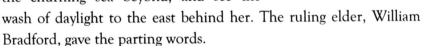

It was July 31, 1620, and the day of departure had come. As they approached the Delft Haven harbor, Mary could hear the churning sea beyond, and see the wash of daylight to the east behind her. The ruling elder, William Bradford, gave the parting words.

"First of all seek heavenly peace with God and your own conscience. Then be at peace with all men as much as possible and not too ready to make offense. Those joining us at Southampton are Strangers, and this may minister continual occasion for offense and

---

[32] **Hewn:** to cut with an ax

be as fuel for fire. Unless you diligently quench it with brotherly forbearance and love, it may spread and consume all. Place the common good before personal advantage. Since ye have no governing official, let wisdom guide us in choosing persons who will promote the common good. After they are chosen, give them all honor and obedience. In Him whom we trust and in whom we rest. Happy success in our hopeful voyage."

Mary opened her arms wide and hugged her sisters, promising one day to welcome them to the New World. Isabella had secretly made a going away gift for Mary.

"Mary, here is a little something for you to remember me by. I hope you like it."

"What can it be?" Mary said with surprise as she carefully unfolded the cloth. All wrapped up in a linen cloth and tied with a string was a small cloth doll. Isabella had used different scraps of fabric and trim from her wealthy customers' gowns. Knowing how limited their space would be, she made sure the tiny doll fit in the palm of Mary's hand and could be kept tucked away inside her skirt pocket.

"Oh, Isabella, 'tis precious and so dear. Thank you, kind sister. I simply adore it!" The two embraced while more gifts were exchanged.

"Mum, this is for you from us girls." Engle gave her mother hand-sewn pouches of lavender.

"And for you, Father," Isabella said. "Here are seedlings and little herbs to plant in the New World all tucked into rich Leyden soil for you to begin a proper garden and to never forget us."

Her sisters had already bid a wrenching farewell to their parents. But with this last offering, all the Chiltons wept openly.

When they reached the boarding ramp, they stood and turned around for one last embrace. Mary's father gave her a gentle pat and kissed her on the top of her head, guiding her to move along. It was a mournful parting. Mary braced herself at the railing while her parents held on to each other waving and waving. There was a wail of anguish from everyone. Mary turned away, as she could not bear to see anyone else's tears. Instead, she held tight to the ropes and looked up to see the billowing sails unfurl. With her head still raised in farewell, she studied the landscape of Delft Haven. On her left, the fields ran down to the sea where they met with the sandy shore. On her right were mature trees standing tall to wish them well. Then there were the sturdy windmills meandering through the air and the timbers of the town pier, which lay upon large rocks. She watched, not wanting to ever forget as the people she loved became tiny glimmers and then vanished altogether across the great North Sea and beyond. She wondered if her friends and family could see her waving in her red frock.

She threw her hands out to balance herself as the ship swayed through the rippling, cold ocean. As she stared at the line of the horizon, clear and hard against the sky, she wondered what lay in that distance far beyond the reach of her imagination where she had never been. It was a whole new world of water. After a bit, Mary realized her father and mother were standing by her side. Father put one arm around her, and another around Mother, and right there on the deck, they bowed their head in prayer, asking God to be their pilot and lead them to a new home in an unknown wilderness. The words warmed Mary's heart and took away some of the sting from the pain of leaving friends and family behind.

As they sailed along, far off in the distance was England. Mary was excited and leaned forward to get a better look at the homeland she had heard so much about.

Down the eastern side of the English coast they sailed, past the pleasant harbor towns of Felixstowe and Harwich, past the wide mouth of the River Thames. Her father directed her attention westward and said, "Mary, notice the coastal village of Dover? Not far over those chalky cliffs is me birthplace, Canterbury. There . . . there! Do ye see them?" Mary could hear the emotion in her father's voice, as if he wanted her to capture the image and keep it in her memory.

Leaning on the railing, she watched the lovely thatched-roof cottages along the seaside, with small farms and villages covering the green hills atop the white cliffs.

"Oh, Father, I wish we could dock here just for a little while," Mary said longingly.

Still pointing, he said with emotion in his voice, "It looks so much like the place we lived before leaving England."

From that day years before, when Father had given her the prized locket, Mary knew that he was sentimental, but seeing his face now as he looked upon his beloved England, she noticed his eyes becoming moist with emotion. It struck her that he felt the same way about leaving England as she felt about leaving Holland. Wishing she could comfort him, she tucked her hand into his and gave a little squeeze.

They had sailed aboard the trusted *Speedwell* from Holland to England, though all too soon they learned the ship was leaking and not seaworthy. Meanwhile, in England, the *Mayflower* had been chartered and waited in the Southampton harbor ready to sail side by side with the *Speedwell*. It was decided, after two attempts to be on their way, that the *Speedwell* would not make the voyage alongside the *Mayflower*. Each time the ships returned to Dartmouth, the late summer heat was fading. These delays and difficulties were of grave concern. Eager to depart, passengers had to endure several weeks of delays before finally leaving from the port in Plymouth, England.

Chapter 8
"Cast Off!"

MARY'S FAMILY WAS AMONG the group chosen to transfer from the *Speedwell* to the *Mayflower*. With the changes from one ship to another, there was a flurry of activity mixed with anxious concern and great excitement as they gathered up all their belongings to shift onto the already crowded *Mayflower*. The Chiltons, along with the other passengers, were required to move quickly. Goodwife Chilton's voice was cheerful, but her face showed her worry over this unexpected change, so Mary tried her best to help her mother prepare for the move. It didn't take long.

"We have everything we need in good order right here in our enormous wooden sea chest.[33] What will this *Mayflower* ship be like, I wonder?" Goodwife Chilton said. Mary shifted her bundle from one hand to the other, helping to keep an eye on their belongings, not wanting anything to get lost or damaged.

"Why not repair the *Speedwell?*" she questioned half aloud.

While waiting their turn to board, Mary's father pointed to the ship and said, "Mary, see the large carved flower design just above the cabin window?" He explained, "In England we would gather this flower on the hills every spring. The mayflower is really the English

---

[33] **Sea chest**: a large shipping trunk

hawthorn that blooms in May, after a frosty winter. That's why they call the ship the *Mayflower*."

"Mum," Mary called, "did ye hear that? See the big flower up there?"

"Aye, Mary, 'tis a flower bearing promise. A hope this ship will bear promise for a safe voyage," her mother uttered under her breath.

Mary held tight to the few precious things that she carried tied up in a blue cotton handkerchief. The sky was full of sunlight, and the ship's great white sails were stiffened by wind. She drew a deep breath of fresh air and watched the family ahead of them in line. According to her father, they were the Mullins. Their oldest daughter, Priscilla, was only a few years older than Mary. With so few girls aboard, Mary was very interested in this young woman. Secretly she was pleased that she would have someone close to her in age who might in time prove to be a friend.

Carrying a pile of linens, Priscilla Mullins led her family aboard the ship. She called for her little brother Joseph to keep up with her and her older parents. "Preserve better walking,[34] else ye could drop clean off the edge of the wharf. Stay close by and step lively."

Mary sat on her family's sea chest, dangling her legs, looking beyond the wharf, where there were street sweepers and flower sellers. Even jugglers and tumblers had come to entertain the people waiting on the wharf. Fascinated, she watched for a bit, then glanced the other way to see a line of crewmen passing heavy sacks from one to the other as they shouted in steady rhythm, "Heave, ho, catch." It looked like hard work as the first mate kept shouting orders to the sailors, urging them to move faster. They all looked like husky, weathered seamen.

---

[34] **"Preserve better walking"**: watch your step

Mary's father brought the last of their bundles. They were only allowed to bring one large sea chest, a Bible box, and what they could carry in their arms. The chest had to contain everything they would need to survive in the New World.

"Why do I have to wear *all* my clothes? 'Tis too hot!" Mary murmured as she pulled up her thick woolen leggings.

Her mother admonished, "While it is August now, ye will be glad you have plenty on when the weather turns cold. Never shall ye forget this blissful feeling of the hot sun on thy back."

"Well, I am plenty warm as it is." Mary was miserable in her layers of clothes, but there was nothing to be done but wait and sweat.

"I have it on good authority the ship is good and sturdy," Mary's father said. "It was used to carry wine but is not actually suited to carry passengers . . . certainly not 102 of them, not to mention fifty sailors and crew, but I am sure that we will all manage."

"Husband, is there room for all of us in that ship?" Mary's mother asked in a worried voice as she observed the crowd.

"Be of good courage, me goodwife.[35] I've learned the ship is ninety feet long and twenty-six feet wide, and we'll have our own place on the 'tween deck—that means between the main deck on top and the hold below." Master Chilton continued on with his newfound information. "The ceiling is only five feet high, so the young people can stand up, but adults will have to bend over to walk. We will be assigned a small space for our family, and we will hang our linens up to create privacy."

Mary saw something out of the corner of her eye. Watching to see if Mary was looking his way, a lively young boy did a flip and

---

[35] **Goodwife:** term used for lower-status women

landed upside down, walking a distance on his hands. She could not resist a quick glimpse. He gave Mary a big grin and a spirited wink and strode off. Mary blinked and turned her head to see if that energetic gesture was meant for someone else. When she realized it wasn't, her cheeks turned pink in a flash.

Just then her father called, "Come, we have precious little time."

Still thinking of that fun-filled lad, Mary picked up her bundles. Father motioned for the family to keep moving forward as they advanced along on the dock, preparing to board.

They heard, "Stand by to loose the fore course sheets."

Father explained that the seaman calling the orders was the bosun.[36]

Mary's mother wearily remarked, "We will soon be underway—we've been waiting many fortnights to start this voyage. My, such a horde of different people. How will we all fit together?"

An odd family with two shameful boys pushing, shoving, and boasting their way up the plank caused people to look the other way with whispered conversations.

A well-fed woman with a roly-poly face squawked, "Get on with ye and carry a load! Move yer feet along, or I'll ring yer necks!" Then, cranking her neck around for approval, she announced, "They aren't worth scat!" She proceeded to mumble to herself as she scuffled along.

The two mousy-haired boys followed behind her, poking and

---

[36] **Bosun**: boatsman

kicking each other. "Gaw! He snatched me pasty.[37] Gimme it back!" whined the shorter boy.

"It's mine!" called the other with his mouth full of something, trying to look as innocent as possible. When he thought no one was looking, he gave a smirk.

Bringing up the rear was their father, a portly, bearded, round-faced man with shifty eyes who began to scratch himself as if his shirt were crawling with fleas and wheezing with every step. He gave a snort of contempt at the bickering boys, slapped them on their heads, tripped over a bundle, and fell with undignified remarks. "Ye hold yer peace, mind ye! I have a cockeyed notion to pop yer heads together!" he bellowed.

"Oh my, such words spoken in anger are never from the heart," Mum said under her breath.

Father came laden with all he could carry. "We're embarking again. Stay close, Mary, so we do not get separated."

As they climbed up the gangplank together, they glanced back over at the *Speedwell* next to them, rocking gently on its mooring with a pleasant swirl of quiet water below. They took nervously to boarding another ship. Some of the children looked excited, and others looked scared.

On the main deck, a handsome young man introduced himself. "Hello, I'm John Alden. May I give ye a hand aboard with your trunk?"

He continued, "I'm the ship's cooper. I've been hired to look after the barrels of food and drink."

"Well done." Mary's father willingly shared the weight of their trunk with John, who asked, "Are ye good people from the Leyden group?"

"Right ye are, young chap." Mary's father welcomed the

---

[37] **Pasty:** a small meat and vegetable pie held in the hand

younger man's help. "Aye, we are from Green Gate, near Leyden. This is me goodwife and me daughter. Thank ye for your assistance."

"The fine summer weather is fast slipping away," John commented cordially, yet with some concern.

"We will reach the New World before the winter storms set in, will we not?" Mary's father asked hopefully.

"I fear not, Goodman." John continued. "Each day of delay adds more worry for a safe voyage. We dare not wait."

He was arranging the barrels of biscuits (hard bread), firkins of butter, all the boxes of Dutch and English cheeses and haberdyne

(dried salted cod), with smoked herring and bacon crowded alongside.

There were big barrels of sauerkraut, potted meat, ham, oatmeal, pease pudding, pickled eggs, sausages, spiced beef, ale, and brandy. Everyone was advised to have plenty of lemon juice to ensure good health. Bags of apples and prunes and casks of olives completed the provisions. With all that they had planned for the voyage, too soon they would run out of provisions; in fact, most of everything. Additional barrels of fresh water were brought over from the *Speedwell*, along with all the slop buckets and barrels that would hold human waste until it could be dumped at sea.

While final plans were being made for military defense in the new colony, Myles Standish, a fearless soldier, climbed aboard with guns and weapons of every sort. As everyone came aboard, the Pilgrims[38] and the Strangers looked each other over and started to get acquainted. The Separatists called themselves "Saints," because they thought of themselves as God's chosen people. Some called them "Puritans," because they wanted to purify the Church and live a life of continuous worship. The others who sailed were strangers to them, so that is what they were called. Few of the passengers had been to sea before. They all had dreams of a better place. Everyone, down to the smallest child, helped by filling their arms full of things that would be needed on the ship and in the New World. Altogether, there were thirty children aboard, with very little space for play. Almost all toys and dolls had to be left behind.

Glancing at a girl next to her, Mary introduced herself. "Hello, my name is Mary. What is your name?"

The girl's answer was almost inaudible. Mary tried again with a smile. "Pardon me, I didn't hear ye."

"Ah, my name is Constance," she answered shyly.

"Me, I'm thirteen years old. How old are ye, Constance?"

"I'm almost the same, though me Mum tells me I'm a mere twelve."

Mary could hardly contain herself, she was so relieved to see another girl her same age. She hoped they would be good friends, perhaps even kindred spirits.

"Unfurl and set the sail!" came the shouts from the ropes above.

Finally, on September 6, 1620, the *Mayflower* set sail.

"Cast off!"[39]

The anchor was finally hoisted up from the bottom of the harbor, and cheers and farewells were heard up and down the wharf

---

[38] **Pilgrim:** someone who goes on a long, long journey
[39] **"Cast off":** lift the anchor

of Plymouth, England. The master of the ship, Captain Christopher Jones, blew a shrill sound with his whistle as the ship slowly moved from the dock. Many people were waving handkerchiefs, and Mary heard the last faint "Godspeed," even the far-off ringing of a church bell, while the earth seemed to glide away from under them to the other side of the horizon. Another wondrous adventure was starting, this time into the vast open sea. The *Mayflower* was a seasoned three-masted, double-decked sailing ship. The ship's timber creaked and groaned as it made its way through the deep waters. Most everyone stood on the top deck for a tearful last good-bye and watched the land of England fade in the distance.

Mary was delighted to learn that there were many children, and even a few dogs, onboard ship. Families found places to get settled with their precious few belongings. Mary cautiously found her way down the narrow ladder leading to the dimly lit 'tween deck, where the passengers would stay.

Her mother called to her, waving her hand, "Mary, I'm over here."

It was so crowded and dark she could hardly find her way. Squinting her eyes, she found the area assigned to her family, where they had spread out and hung their lengths of linen. Their quilt coverlet looked too delicate to be trodden upon by rough feet, but Mary was glad to see something familiar in their little corner where she could lay her head.

"Where is Father?" Mary looked around in concern.

"He is with the boys and menfolk. Mothers and children are at this end for now, and most all the men will be at the other end."

This felt odd to Mary, because she and her mother had always relied on the guidance and strength of her father. She told herself he was only a short walk away, but their corner suddenly seemed lonelier.

"Look, Mary, our space is next to this tiny window near the stern where it will give us some daylight and a bit of fresh air."

Mary's mother always tried to make the best of their situation. Mary glanced around and saw Constance with her mother, Goodwife Hopkins, who was large with child.

"I'm sorry it is a small space, but it will not be for long—three, four weeks at the most," Goodwife Hopkins cheerfully said.

Just then, Mary's father appeared, trying to accustom himself to the movement of the vessel. "All settled? Are ye comfortable? Looks like ye have pleasant company."

"Father, this is the Hopkins family, and Constance is my new friend," Mary said with a smile. After her father bade them good day and returned to the men's side of the deck, Mary and Constance remained together, sharing thoughts and stories. Mary was proud of her father. She told Constance, "My father is a tailor and hopes to have a shop in the new colony."

Constance replied in her soft, thin voice, "Me father hopes to have a tavern." She smiled at Mary and said, "Having a friend will be so nice. We are the very same age, well, almost."

Squeezing together and adjusting to their new surroundings, the Separatists quickly became acquainted with the Strangers and other more notable passengers.

Mary told Constance, "We are not just saints and not just strangers, but I like better the word Master William Bradford did make up for us. We are all 'Pilgrims.'"

"I like the word *Pilgrim*; it is a word that brings us together and fits us all," Constance said.

"Constance, have ye bid many friends good-bye in England?"

"Aye, one never really knows how much one has been touched by a place or friends until one has to leave. I did shed many tears. And ye, Mary?"

"Aye, I feel that my body is in one place and my soul is still in Green Gate." Images flashed through Mary's thoughts: Remy laughing as he chased her to the top of the dike; Master Albert purring in her arms; the lovely little bedroom in the windmill castle. It was painful to think about her friends and family and pet, somewhere under the same sun but forever out of reach.

"We will not have an easy time of it, yet me Mum always says 'Ye are not to sit in the shade of life,' so here we are, setting out to sea on a golden sunny day," Constance cheerfully added.

The girls were startled when a loud voice interrupted them. "Pipe down, ye rotten scamps!" Mary soon realized the angry words weren't directed at her and Constance. Heads turned as they heard a woman holler back in a snarly voice, "I have no mind to bother with ye now. Now, shoo, or I'll box yer ears good and hard!"

"Mercy me," Mary's mother said. "What kind of a voyage will it be with them so nearby?"

Others shook their heads in disgust. "Who are those dirty, worthless boys?" Mistress[40] Mullins asked.

Soon everyone knew each other's names, including that of the rude family. They were the Billington family. Everyone wondered how this family, so profane and disrespectful toward others and religion, had shuffled into their company.

"Fortunately, their place is at the other end of the ship," Mary's mother said with a sigh.

Others who were more annoyed spoke out with less tolerance. "Take a good grip, the voyage is a lengthy one!"

There were shopkeepers, tradesmen, and farmers. The colonists came from many regions and spoke an assortment of dialects.[41] Some knew how to read, while others did not. Some families

---

[40] **Mistress**: term used for wealthy women
[41] **Dialect**: a variety of a spoken language

brought servants, but most did not. No one regarded themselves as a group of equals.

"All up on deck!" A call came from William Brewster, and the humble group of Leyden exiles gathered with their heads bowed and their hands together in prayer.

"On this day of departure, September 6th, 1620, let us seek heavenly peace with God . . ."

After Elder Brewster's prayer, the good saints began to sing the hymn "Old One Hundredth." Mary joined in and softly sang along with everyone:

> All people that on earth do dwell,
> Sing to the Lord with cheerful voice.
> Him serve with fear, His praise forth tell;
> Come ye before Him and rejoice.
>
> The Lord, ye know, is God indeed;
> Without our aid He did us make;
> We are His folks, He doth us feed,
> And for His sheep He doth us take.
>
> Oh enter then His gates with praise
> Approach with joy His courts unto;
> Praise, laud, and bless His Name always,
> For it is seemly so to do.
>
> For why? The Lord our God is good;
> His mercy is forever sure;
> His truth at all times firmly stood,
> And shall from age to age endure.
> To Father, Son and Holy Ghost,

The God Who Heav'n and Earth adore,
From men and from the angel host
Be praise and glory evermore.
Amen.

All at once, orders filled the air.

"Unfurl the sails!"

"Men aloft!"

Seamen began hauling on the lines, and the rigging snapped as the sailors climbed barefoot up the ropes. Suddenly, a strong wind picked up, and the ship began to speed along with a soft thunder of breaking waves against the bow.

While others were up on deck for prayer, some of the Strangers below took advantage by spreading their belongings out and taking up more space.

"Not enough elbow room down here," someone mumbled loud enough so everyone could hear. Everyone needed to cooperate and respect one another. Within a fortnight, Elder William Bradford could see right away a need to call the passengers together.

"Although we have our differences," he began, "we are all God's children, and as such we are but specks in the vastness of this ocean, but precious unto our Lord. Now, together we are voyagers, Pilgrims, and look to thine infinite mercy and providence."

At long last they settled in. Right away, the children invented fun games played wherever they could find space to spread out. One of their favorites was hide-and-seek. They created their own amusements by making a pattern with string or yarn around their fingers called cat's cradle and making dolls out of rags or just playing finger games.

A few exploring youngsters were firmly hauled down out of the lower rigging and warned away from the ship's sails by scolding mothers who quickly settled them down before the sailors could get their hands on them. "Shame, shame. Do ye see the folly of it all?" Then their mothers took them below.

John Alden, the cooper, showed how to whittle a puzzle from some of the wooden barrel staves, and a few of the boys were taught how to tie knots by some of the kinder, younger sailors. Only a few of them were nice; many of the sailors were crude and terribly mean. Because every inch of the ship was crowded with a multitude of smells and tight spaces, it wasn't long before it sent Mary up the ladder and through the hatch. The scent of old cheese, hardtack biscuits, dried meat, and baskets of wilted vegetables cramped in with barrels of ale made her stomach turn.

"I need fresh air!" she desperately explained. She leaned over the rail to watch the foam whipped up by the bow forging through the waves. Everyone needed room to stretch and clean air to breath, but that was not always possible, even though there was hardly a place to put their feet. The *Mayflower* had no heat. Even worse, there were no toilets except buckets, which took the place of chamber pots that had to be emptied overboard at least twice a day! Mary didn't like to be cooped up down below under the main deck of the ship, so whenever she could, she would slip out of the 'tween deck, even though it wasn't the safest thing to do, and go up for a fresh breath of air.

Constance, her new friend, joined her, and they leaned over the rail together. On this particular day, the ocean was fairly calm. The ship pitched as the bow cut though the waves. The air was balmy, with not a cloud in the sky. They could see the dark churning water far below. Being drenched occasionally with ocean spray added to their adventure. Several sailors nearby engaged in their various tasks, which they didn't interrupt to even glance at the new passengers. In fact, the crew considered the passengers simply as part of the cargo. Never idle, the topmen were responsible for the masts, while the rest of the sailors worked the lower sails and took turns at the wheel. The sail-man knew all there was to know about sails. A ship must be tended to day and night. Most of the crew were rough men with little patience for each other, let alone passengers.

Captain Jones's eyes would flash like steel when he gave orders on the *Mayflower*. But his eyes softened when he looked into the eyes of a Pilgrim child. Mary looked up with wonderment at the main mast jutting into the sky. Captain Jones looked at the two girls with a furrowed brow for a moment. It was a look that filled Mary with concern and perhaps a little anticipation. She did not wish to be in trouble with the captain of the ship, but she could not take her eyes off of his bushy eyebrows. The ship was well underway and he could spare a few moments. He routinely took his pipe from his pocket, and he gave a merry chuckle as he filled his pipe, looking out to sea. It was clear that this was his world and he didn't want any other.

The captain's face was weathered from the salty air and wind, and his eyes, though piercing, softened as he spoke. He squinted at these Pilgrim girls and raised his eyebrows at the same time. The captain smiled with amusement as Mary timidly asked a question.

"I beg your pardon, sir," she said, pulling herself together in an effort to stand without losing her balance. "Ye must think me rude, but may I ask why there are so many ropes?"

The captain gave a quick, playful wink. "Aye, 'tis many, fifty or more, and each has a proper purpose to make the ship move along."

Mary caught the twinkle in his eye. Sometimes Mary wished she were a boy and could explore and climb the entire ship from bow to stern, but girls were expected to keep their place and tend to things like needlework.

Mary felt like Captain Jones thought well of her by the way he spoke to her as if she were an adult. By now a few other children gathered and came along. He put a protective arm around Mary as he guided the inquisitive little group. His hands were large and strong with calluses on the palms. He showed the children different parts of the ship and pointed to the crow's nest above and the starboard below. Mary enjoyed hearing all about the ship.

"The main mast and crow's nest are above the poop deck. The half deck and rudder are below. The shallop[42] is a longboat we use to row ashore for emergencies. 'Tis the best kind of small boat to explore the coastline. At the very front of the ship is the spritsail and beak bow. The more wind in her sails, the faster we will move out."

Mary was spellbound and repeated quietly to herself the various parts of the ship. Captain Jones said, "Ye learn quickly. I think we are all off to a good start."

"'Tis a jolly life being at sea!" she responded.

"So 'tis, so 'tis," he said with great heartiness, but even as he showed the children around the *Mayflower,* he was always keeping an eye on the function and task of the ship.

Mary responded with a slight curtsy, "I had hoped for thy good pleasure, thank thee, Master—I mean Captain Jones."

Right then and there, the small group of children who had tagged along thought Mary to be bold-spirited and fascinating! Captain Jones motioned for the children to move aside—his attention was suddenly on the upper sails near the crow's nest.

---

[42] **Shallop**: an open boat fitted with oars, or sails, or both; the shallop on the *Mayflower* had both and was large enough to hold approximately sixteen adult persons.

The Captain kept the ship on course by using a magnetic compass and a cross-staff. He measured the speed of the *Mayflower* with a ship log. The gentle rocking from side to side became stronger, and all of a sudden clouds opened up and the sky burst with heavy rain that became a torrential downpour splashing on the deck. The children were frightened; it was no longer a safe place for them.

Mary reached out for Constance, yelling against the wind, "Hurry, let's go down below!"

"A storm is coming yonder," Captain Jones shouted to his crew. "Be quick! We must mark our course well. This is likely to be rough."

He no longer had time for children and ordered them to find shelter. "Get on with it. All of ye go below!" he commanded.

They all made haste to return below.

The autumn gales began to blow. Mary glanced back to see the young sailors scramble with their tough bare feet up the lines to adjust the sails. The awkward lines were sticky with tar so they wouldn't lose their grip.

Captain Jones called out, "There will be no steering the ship during the storm. We will drift in the hands of God." Mary's father had explained why storms at sea were so deadly. With the wind blowing the ship in the same direction as the waves, steering became next to impossible. They would be at the mercy of the wind until the storm passed.

The sailors above worked the heavy sails.

Mary scurried down the hatch stairs to be met with shouts and confusion.

"Douse your cooking fire and all lanterns and candle sticks!"

"Secure all that is likely to roll about!"

"The hatch will be covered until the waves calm!"

"Be brave!"

Above her, Mary could hear Captain Jones even over the howling gale. He cried, "Everyone stay below deck!"

Obediently, everyone hurried to find a secure place as the storm mounted to a new fury. The sea seemed to be holding its breath, as though it were waiting for something awful to happen.

"Secure the hatches!"[43] was Captain Jones's final call.

---

[43] **Hatch:** a door to the tween deck or other decks below

Chapter 9
The 'Tween Deck

THE WAVES THREW WATER everywhere, and the small window in the Chilton's corner let in gushes of water before they could finally close the latch.

"Fair weather has faded too soon," Mary heard her mother quietly murmur.

They could hear the sailors running to and fro and the mates shouting orders above the wind.

Mary was feeling queasy, like she might cast up the contents of her stomach at any moment. She curled up on the rough wood floor of the deck and made a pillow out of one corner of a rough woolen blanket. The rest of the blanket she wrapped around her shoulders as best she could to keep the chill at bay. She listened to the conversations of those around her.

Goodwife Hopkins looked fair ill as she spoke. "With this confinement, the heavy stench presses upon me."

Goodwife Chilton came over to her aid. "If we had a bit of air, 'twould give some relief down here."

Mistress Mullins added, holding her nose, "Now then, pishposh! I call it simply mindless. Could not Captain Jones let us push the hatch open just a wee bit for some decent air?"

Mary closed her eyes tight and faintly listened in the darkness to the orders topside. She took deep breaths so she wouldn't heave. Priscilla Mullins, who was eighteen years old, braced herself against the wall of the ship and tried to brush the tangles from her long auburn hair. Mary had overheard some of the older women murmuring that Priscilla had too much vanity[44] and that she was frippery with wearing ribbons under her coif and such. But Mary liked her. Priscilla seemed calm and good-natured, and always had a smile for Mary and the other children.

"Surely Captain Jones should never wish us harm, but his crewmen are a different lot, rather fearsome," Priscilla spoke up.

Holding on to one of the great beams that supported the upper deck with both hands for balance, Constance joined the conversation. "If you wish to be modest, the 'tween deck is not the place to be. To change me petticoat, I practically have to hide behind the crates and fishing traps."

Priscilla agreed. "The men are less modest than the women." She continued on another subject. "Oh, it's all very well to talk and converse, but I am weary of being cramped below and hearing the loud snores of Master Billington," she said rather pettishly.

Someone in the dark let out a suppressed complaint. "As well as Mistress Billington! She makes a sound through her nose like a pitch pipe!"

Mary was too sick to listen or speak anymore. She arranged herself in her narrow hammock, which curled about her like a peapod. The crashing waves rocked the ship back and forth, and the

---

[44] **Vanity:** being too proud of oneself

gossip faded into a muffled lull. How she missed her stuffed feather pillow and her light-filled bedchamber in the windmill. She felt for her locket and held it tight. Desperately trying not to vomit, she took a deep breath and murmured the engraved saying. "Sweet are the uses of adversity." *Sweet? Honey is sweet, but I find nothing sweet about this,* she thought as she shivered from the dampness in the dark. Her mother and father were trying to get settled.

"Keep taking nice deep breaths, Mary," her mother said. "Do not be frightened."

At that very moment the ship took a violent lunge in the fierce winds, throwing the entire 'tween deck into a state of shock from the jerk and bounce.

Mary was suddenly flung into the air where her arm got twisted in the ropes of the hammock, burning her wrist. She was bruised and aching, plus her face was red and chapped from windburn. Her mother rubbed it with a mixture of herbs and animal fat to sooth the pain.

"Are we all going to die?" Mary wondered out loud.

"I do not think ye are to worry about that," her father answered, laying a gentle hand on her head.

Usually her father's deep, calm voice would have reassured her, but now Mary heard something in his tone that made her stomach drop more than the tossing of the ship. Fear. Father was scared. But he would never say it. And Mary realized she wouldn't either. She must be brave for her mother and father. But hearing the tone in her father's voice filled Mary with worry. Thoughts swirled around in her head. Her childhood, her true friendships, her big sisters, her sweet Albert, and her carefree sense of security—all of these things seemed to be slipping away from her grasp. With her new heightened fears, she was overwhelmed, but her labored breathing and throbbing arm seemed to take her seasickness away, at least for a while. Mary's father helped her back into her hammock where she knew very well, in spite of what the captain had told them, only a narrow wall rested between them and the vast, angry sea. Soon her eyes closed and she was finally asleep.

During the storm, the salty seawater soaked the main deck and dripped down below onto the Pilgrims. The air was already thick with the smell of spoiled food, sickness, and unwashed bodies. Some of the Pilgrims who were sick often vomited on themselves or their neighbors. Unexpectedly, people were thrown about from side to side. Seasickness became like a plague.

In a blur of nausea and misery, Mary overheard the captain shouting above deck, "The gales are hitting us head on! The craft is wallowing bravely through the overpowering swells!"

Then even louder he yelled, "They threaten to swamp us!"

Frigid temperatures hit overnight. The cold penetrated every crack and cranny of the *Mayflower* as winds began tearing and clawing at the vessel. With most everyone sick, they stayed confined in the dark to their bunks and swaying hammocks.

By morning the sea was calm again, and some passengers climbed up on the main deck and hung pale and limp on the deck rail simply to take in some clean, unpolluted air. Mary lay for a while in silence, watching the shadows of the hanging beds move slowly in the still air. What a relief that the pitching of the ship had ceased and with it, her illness. With all the noise and excitement during the stormy night, she hadn't heard the moans of Goodwife Hopkins or cries of a newborn baby, so it was a surprise when Constance rushed to her side.

"Mary, Mary, happy news! Me Mum's baby is here! Come and see the wee one."

Forgetting the trauma of the all-night storm, Mary hastily turned over, slipped out of her hammock, and quickly followed

Constance, forgetting her shoes in the excitement. Everyone heard the news and wanted a peek at this Pilgrim baby who was born in the middle of the stormy sea!

Mary stumbled through the darkness after Constance, pushing aside quilts, belongings, baskets, and jugs to make room to catch a glimpse of the newest passenger. She heard, "'Tis a boy!"

"We shall name him Oceanus," his father announced. Cheers filled the passageway.

Mary knelt beside the wicker cradle. "Oh my, hello, Oceanus, you are a dear little lad! What a tiny creature to ride out such a storm. "Ye are an awfully brave chap."

She was enchanted when Oceanus curled his tiny hand around her finger. Was there any feeling so tender and sweet?

Constance watched her baby brother affectionately. "Angels brought him carefully to us through the night."

Mary removed her hand from his and patted his little head and, with Constance, sat quietly beside the cradle taking in this new life of a tiny soul.

Elder Brewster calmly spoke. "We shall welcome this newest Pilgrim with a prayer of gratitude."

Mary tried but could not concentrate on the prayer, not when her thoughts were full of baby Oceanus. She even snuck a peek at him, then quickly closed her eyes as she remembered the times Elder Brewster had told the children again and again that they offended God when they allowed their thoughts to stray while in prayer. Elder Brewster's prayer was so long that she was pleased when she heard Master Mullins clear his throat twice. She knew then that there were two of them who had grown impatient. Just then everyone said, "Amen."

In the mist of the passageway, Mary's mother worked side by side with the other women. It was natural work to them as they supervised the cooking, for women were expected to solely occupy their time caring for children and husbands. They visited as they prepared a meal of corned pork and cooked cabbages in a kettle suspended over the sand hearth—a metal box filled with sand in which a small charcoal fire could be built during calm seas. When the sea was choppy they could not use the sand hearth for fear of fire. Most of the meals were served cold.

One afternoon, young Joseph Mullins fled to his mother crying,

"Francis and John Billington said they are going to toss me overboard! I need to hide quickly."

He promptly dove into the folds of his mother's skirts.

"Stop fretting, Joseph, you are safe enough here." His mother's eyes flashed as she raised her arm and said shortly, "Well, I never! Those boys are headed for trouble. Heaven help that family!"

Another older woman said, exasperated, while shaking her head, "Been up to their sneaky pranks again, them boys!"

"Mary, the children are unsettled and hungry. A lively story would amuse them. Please engage them until supper is ready," her mother implored.

Mary called out the children's names, "Joseph! Samuel! Humility! Remember! Blessing! Come gather around." One tiny wisp of a girl hung back in the shadows. She could have been no more than three or four. Mary beckoned her to come and sit by her side. "What is thy name, wee one?" With wide eyes that looked a little lost, she whispered, "Mary More." The name was one Mary had overheard when the adults talked in hushed whispers of the four More siblings. The More children were traveling alone as indentured servants for three other families. No wonder the wee girl looked so sad. Hard as it had been to leave her sisters, Mary couldn't imagine being so far from her father and mother. If only she could cheer the moppet up.

"Why, that is my name too. Two Marys. However will people tell us apart?" Mary's teasing worked, for a slow smile crept over the child's face.

Each one brought another little friend. Joseph wiggled in the middle and sat cross-legged, glad he could double his legs under him. Children often learned to read from the Bible as families studied it together daily. The Word was the world to them—it was full of drama, poetry, and mystery. Mary's father had brought an almanac[45] and a small chapbook[46] of stories, songs, and rhymes.

"Who has a fine riddle to share?" Mary started out. "Or, who would care to tell us a fine scripture from the Bible?"

As more children joined the group, Mary collected her thoughts and began one of Aesop's fables. "Long ago there was a proud, strong oak tree and a humble water reed. They would often talk. The oak boasted of his strength. The reed replied that she was content with her lot. One day a fierce storm arose and uprooted the mighty oak. But the humble reed weathered the storm because she was able to bend with the wind."

Sitting straight up, the children took to every word. They were forbidden to run and had to endure long hours in close quarters during bad weather. Some of their favorite games were Nine Men's Morris, a board game, pick-up sticks, and marbles. But they learned that a story told by Mary was the best favor of all.

---

[45] **Almanac:** a calendar with astronomical data, weather forecasts, etc.
[46] **Chapbook:** a book with chapters

The children's attention was completely on the story, but Mary was aware of the women speaking in worried tones just beyond the story circle. "Our food supplies are getting low. The rye bread is all but gone. We have some pork fat, cheese, and raw onions, but the parsnips, cabbages, and turnips are turning soft with dreadful mold. Tomorrow it will be a scanty supper," Mistress Mullins informed the women in an anxious voice.

"Pease pottage can be served hot or cold and we can add more water to the porridge," Mary's mother, a soup expert, responded with a more hopeful tone.

The women talked about how to make the spoiled and moldy food taste better. Spices such as cinnamon, ginger, and nutmeg would help cover up the bad taste of rotting food, and more salt in the gruel[47] would make the belly feel full.

"What the eye can't see the heart won't grieve over," expressed another.

In the light of the oil lamp, the children's faces glowed. They clustered around Mary as she told them more stories from her imagination. As she glanced beyond the heads of the children, she was distracted for a moment—a lad stood off to the side in the very back of the 'tween deck watching her with a grin on his face.

He seemed so familiar.

Then her attention went back again to the children. Soon they all began to smell the cooked cabbage. Their stomachs were empty, and they began to chatter about food.

Mary promptly asked, "What is your favorite morsel of food?"

Again her eyes strayed to the strange boy, but she could no longer see him. Each of the children had their own favorites.

"I like sweet bread with butter."

---

[47] **Gruel:** a thin soup

"Doughboys."

"Plum duff."

"Burgoo,"[48] said another.

"Me mum makes burgoo or thick hasty pudding[49] all fluffy and full of cinnamon, and I eat every smidgen."

"Oh, ye are all making me hungry!" Mary exclaimed. "We will have a grand feast one day when we shall have a large spoonful of warm milk again."

"Aye!" all the children happily agreed.

A loud voice behind her said, "Yorkshire pudding[50] hot from the pan is me favorite, what is yours?"

Taken by surprise, Mary spun around. It was the boy with the cheeky grin.

At that moment, he cleared his throat. "Are ye one of them Saints from Leyden?"

"Aye," Mary politely said, still set back a bit on her heels.

"Me name is John Hooke, but everyone calls me Johnny. I am Master Allerton's servant boy."

By now the children had run to their mums for their portion of food.

Mary remembered something. "Are ye the lad who did a flip and walked on your hands at the Plymouth port?"

They grinned at each other and chuckled.

"Aye, and I can well fancy ye are Mary."

A bit embarrassed, Mary quickly glanced downward. How did he know her name?

To take the attention off of herself, Mary asked, "What part of England did ye come from?"

---

[48] **Burgoo:** oatmeal
[49] **Hasty pudding:** cornmeal mush
[50] **Yorkshire pudding:** batter baked in meat drippings

"My family came to Holland from Norwich. 'Tis the city of me birth, though no more. Now me home is the *Mayflower* or any pleasant port between here and wilderness of a new colony!"

Just then Mary's mother joined them. "And Johnny, who are your kinfolk?"

"Oh, I have none. Been an orphan since a wee lad," Johnny replied.

"Well then . . ." Mary's Mum paused, looking ill at ease. "'Tis a sad lot when such things happen."

Mary was suddenly tongue-tied. But Johnny shrugged as if he had no cares. Goodwife Chilton said, "Mary, we need your help with the mending."

Mary wanted to stay and visit with Johnny, but there would be plenty of time yet on their journey for that. She bid him good day and went to gather up some socks to be darned.

Goodwife Chilton looked around and asked with a slightly accusing tone, "And where is Priscilla?"

Mistress Mullins sensed a bit of judgment and rather defensively spoke up, "Priscilla, ye see, is already occupied with mending."

"Oh, of course." Mary's mother changed the subject before any hard feelings could flare into an argument. "Lately I have noticed she certainly has the attention of that handsome John Alden, a hopeful young man. Has he taken a fancy to her?" she asked.

"Aye, he certainly finds reasons to come down and see how she is fairing," Mistress Mullins agreed. "She sits and waits, doing her needle work, yet when he appears her face shows an outward glow and she struggles to cover her blushing."

"Aye, I think there's a bit of romance in the air," responded Mary's mother.

And then she continued, "Everyone will have their day of bliss and glory."

Mistress Mullins quickly added, "But 'tis best . . . not to count your eggs before they are in the pudding!"

Knowing that they had many days and hours of working side by side, the women made an effort to be congenial and pleasant with each other. Mending was usually not Mary's favorite task, but she enjoyed listening to the conversations around her.

Moments later, Mistress Mullins exclaimed, "Oh my, such a sound! Master and Mistress Billington are in the midst of a terrible feud. They bicker back and forth speaking in loud whispers, thinking to spare everyone their noise."

"But not for long. Did ye hear that? She can screech as loud as the wind!" Goodwife Chilton exclaimed.

"And he with his curses!" Priscilla sat up and joined in.

"While most fathers read the Bible and explain it to their children's understanding, the Billingtons pay precious little notice to their boys' mishaps." Another said scornfully, "Don't they have a thimble full of brains?"

Even louder now and coming closer, with a red nose and food hanging in his beard, was Master Billington, still berating his wife. "Gaw, don't give me the rough side of yer tongue! Hold your gab!"

"Ah, ye keep a civil tongue in yer mouth, or I'll pop ye one!"

The loud, rough language flew freely across the 'tween deck.

Master Mullins responded sarcastically, "Now, that sounds proper respectful!"

The Pilgrims cupped hands over their children's ears and shushed the Billingtons to regain peace for the sake of everyone.

"Hush, for the sake of the children," a woman nearby promptly added.

"Aye, and their boys are ever watchful for an opportunity to make trouble for others," Mistress Mullins added under her breath.

"They have spared the rod and spoiled the child. Those lads

need a good whipping," Mary's mother whispered, shaking her head and turning away.

"Such profanity," Goodwife Hopkins offered in disbelief.

"Topside 'tis worse," Priscilla said with disgust in her voice.

"One sailor is especially profane and bullies all the Saints, making fun of our prayers and songs," Mary piped in. "And they call us 'glib-glabbety' and when we are seasick, 'puke stockings,' but Captain Jones says I have my sea legs now and that I look pert."

"Well, stay clear of those sailors, Mary. They have a large number of odd taboos, and none like to sail on a ship that carries women," Priscilla said.

"Well if that isn't a bunch of malarkey! Thinking we bring bad luck to their ship and its crew. Hmph." Goodwife Hopkins spoke right up.

"Aye, they are a sneaky, rotten bunch," Mistress Mullins added, pinching her nose together, "With yellow teeth, ill-smelling breath, and their language is even more filthy!"

Priscilla sat upright and with a bit of authority in her voice reported, "Well, John Alden told me the whole lot of them have lived a hard seaman's life."

Constance, who had been taking it all in, said, "Seems to me they need a few of our prayers in their behalf."

"I don't know if prayers would even help," Priscilla said with a good amount of spirit. "One old sailor is enormous. Why, his neck is thicker than his head, and he's got large knuckles and hair all the way up his arms to his face. These contemptible crews are less concerned with the passengers and speak with little respect. If they could, they would stand by with delight and watch us die one by one."

Young Constance gasped as she got an earful of the colorful gossip. Mary glanced at her friend, her own heart racing at the thought of such wickedness, nor was she able to think of another word to add to the squall of spreading stories.

Away from all the scuttlebutt and while they could still catch some light from the small window, Mary and Constance sat to do their needlework.

"Sometimes when I work my needle in and out I think how this tiny object, so easily misplaced, has helped our humble family along the way and provided us with butter on the table and shoes on our feet," Mary said.

"I agree, Mary, a needle is a good woman's skill."

"Constance, have you ever given thought to how boys get to know how to read and write and cipher[51] and girls have to be quietly occupied with needle and thread?" Mary asked, half annoyed with the notion.

"Well, Mary, we do learn letters and numbers as we stitch them into our samplers, do we not?"

"I suppose so. My older sisters are experts with needles. Isabella, my sister, made a little going-away doll for me." Reaching into her underskirt pocket where she kept her hidden treasures, Mary pulled out her tiny doll. "Would you like to hold it?"

Constance admired the detail of the petite sleeves and the little trim on the wee frock.

"Look at those tiny eyes made from French knots. What a dear keepsake," she said.

"I do cherish it." Mary tucked it back into her pocket.

"To stitch so precisely would be a gift," Constance noted.

"Indeed, but I simply don't wish to have it my whole ambition in life," Mary took another good look at her sampler and placed it on her lap.

---

[51] **Cipher:** to solve arithmetic problems

"Constance, do ye know who Johnny Hooke is?"

"No, I don't believe I do. Who is he?"

Mary grew more animated as she talked. "I've been noticing him—he is around our age and has quite a wit. He came with Master Allerton from Leyden, but I didn't notice him until we reached London."

"So he is aboard our ship?" Constance wanted to know everything.

Just as Mary began to tell her more, Priscilla approached them.

"Shh—I shall tell ye later," Mary became quiet as a clam.

"Oh my, both of ye are doing fine work." Admiring Mary's needlework, she expressed, "May I take note of your samplers?"

The two friends exchanged looks of surprise. They didn't think Priscilla would ever bother to speak to them directly, or even take notice, for that matter. Mary always tried extra hard to spy the ribbons Priscilla concealed in her hair, under her coif. Secretly, Mary thought it was cunning and that it was probably how her own sisters dressed their hair in Holland. Once, Mary had overheard Priscilla say that John Alden was the delight of her eye and the darling of her heart. Even though she was only a few years older than them, the girls thought she was more like a refined woman who was polished and cultured. And besides, she'd attracted the eye of fair John Alden.

"What does yours say, Mary?"

Mary stopped daydreaming and held up her sampler. Wanting to impress Priscilla, she began to recite haltingly from memory, a bit self-conscious since she did not know how to read a single word.

Mary Chilton . . . is my name . . . Lord
guide my heart . . . that I may . . . do thy will.
Also fill . . . my hands with . . . such convenient skill

as may conduce to . . . virtue void of shame
and I will give glory to . . . thy name.

"That is a lovely expression. Your needle work is clean and accurate."

Mary blushed. No one had ever remarked on her needlework before.

"And yours, Constance?"

Just as she began to share her sampler they were interrupted by loud voices.

"Ouch!" Startled, Mary stuck herself with her needle.

Above was commotion and scrambling. "Man overboard!" came the shouts. A fear came over the girls.

"Overboard . . . has someone fallen off the ship?"

Terror spread throughout the 'tween deck.

Mary asked, "How can anyone survive if they fall into that ocean?"

Her mother said, "Dear Lord, let him be saved, whoever it might be."

As they waited to hear any news, there was great despair among the passengers.

Soon they learned that it was John Howland who had gone up on deck for fresh air and accidently slipped on some rope, causing him to fall under the railing into the sea. The crew were of little help as they cried out, "Gone!"

"Washed away!"

"Nowhere in sight!"

In spite of their jeers, many hands frantically reached out to rescue the man.

One sailor was heard saying with a booming reply, "Aye, one less prayin' Pilgrim to deal with!"

Several of the stronger men from the 'tween deck had hurried topside as soon as the news was heard, to see if they could help. The rest of the passengers could do nothing but wait fearfully for news.

The worst was expected, and then all at once came good news.

"Alive!"

"God be praised!"

It was young Johnny Hooke who brought the good news. Word quickly passed through the 'tween deck below. Mary joined the crowd of people pressing in around Johnny to hear his story. "I saw him lose his balance and fall!" he began, and the whole tale came out. After slipping into the turbulent water, John had grabbed at the first thing that came to his hand—a bit of rope trailing from the topsail. The lively young man, a servant of John Carver's family, had hung on for his life, even when he'd been dragged under the water for many terrifying moments. Finally his fellow Pilgrims had been able to get a boat hook around him and pulled him onto the slippery deck.

The bosun, who was the sailing master, had pronounced in a routine fashion, "Even though half frozen, he will live! He went under the water some fathoms[52] during the course!"

Soon John Howland was carried below, shivering and unconscious.

"Fetch a basin to dress his cuts with sticking plaster," Elder Brewster requested, and gave him some of his ration[53] of strong water. The first officer offered a heavy woolen covering. "From the captain," he said and handed it over to Elder Brewster.

There was much concern realizing that the heartless sailors neither cared nor lifted a hand to help. Some had actually looked the other way. Everyone worried that if such an accident like this

---

[52] **Fathom**: a length of six feet, used to measure nautical depth
[53] **Ration**: restricted amount of food or water

could happen with an adult, then certainly a helpless child was in more danger and even more powerless. Just thinking about it left Mary with a cold knot in her stomach.

"We pulled him out of the frigid water with the effort of one sailor and the Elders," John Alden announced with relief.

Mary overheard Elder Mullins announce, "By the grace of God, he will live."

Mary and Constance remained below caring for Oceanus and the other little ones, anxious to hear more details. With relief everyone humbly offered a prayer of gratitude to God above.

Mary put her hand on her chest, feeling for her locket, and held it in her fist.

Constance had noticed it before. "Your gold locket is such a pretty thing. May I see it?"

"Aye, but I don't wish to take it off."

Constance studied it carefully.

"It has something engraved on it," she said with curiosity.

Mary began to tell about her grandmother, her suffering, her life of trouble and woe, and how, at the end of her life, she was a stronger and better person.

"Father says that there can be much compensation for suffering and hardship. My locket says, 'Sweet are the uses of adversity.'"

"Imagine that," Constance said respectfully. "What a fine little treasure."

Mary nodded, still giving lingering thought to the engraving and its mysterious saying. The sound of a familiar voice made her perk up, and she squinted her eyes, straining through the dim light.

"Oh no, Constance, it's him!" Mary gave her friend a sudden jab with her elbow to catch her attention. Mary's first impulse was to turn and go the other way, but Constance giggled and nudged her back.

"Mary of the *Mayflower*, cheers!"

The two girls looked at each other and exchanged a grin. Johnny's eyes wandered past Mary to Constance.

"Johnny, this is my friend, Constance."

A smile flashed across his face as he glanced back at Mary. He removed his cap, "Pleased."

"Ye are soaked!" Mary said.

"Aye, John Alden and I helped the others pull John Howland back up. He fell overboard, ye know."

"What a fright," Constance replied.

"Aye, he's a lucky chap. There's not many that could survive a swim like that, with the sea in winter's grip. He will be fine." Johnny was fidgety, twisting water from his cap.

Mary's stomach rumbled horribly loud in the brief silence. Mortified, she could only burst into an embarrassed giggle and make light of it. She shrugged her shoulders, saying with an impish grin, "Suppose 'tis time for a hearty meal!"

Mary was desperately hungry but strived to conceal it and nodded with half approval when her mum offered Johnny a mug of pottage.

"Give it a go!" Mary said, her eyes fixed on the mug.

"Sorry 'tis cold to the taste," apologized Goodwife Chilton. "All ye men and boys who helped save John Howland need a trifle more solids in thy bellies."

"Hot or cold is fine with me. I thank ye." He promptly took the stone-cold pottage and slurped it in one gulp, obviously not certain when he would eat again.

He wiped his mouth with the back of his hand. "Did ye get a swig[54] of this gruel, Mary?"

"Nay, there's no need," she said, lying a little.

---

[54] **Swig:** a sip

He tipped his hat to them and was on his way.

"Why, did ye see that? He jolly smacked his lips at that pottage. I'm so famished, I'd munch on anything to quiet me pangs in me belly. He was obviously more anxious about the rescue than he'd admit," her mother said.

Privately, Mary agreed. The edge of her hunger was something fierce. The memory of her mother's soup washed over her. What she would have given for just one sip.

"All that helped in the deliverance of John Howland got a cup of soup," Mary said. "I'm strong, and could help in such a crisis . . . then I'd get me some supplement too, something to stick to me ribs."

Even boiled herring, which she did not like one bit, sounded good to her.

Her mother responded with a patient nod. "Aye, be long-suffering, me dear. I have never seen such rags on a boy. His woolen doublet and knickers are patched and frayed. I pity the lad," Mary's mother dolefully added and turned back to clean the galley.

Chapter 10
"Be Ye Warned!"

THE NEXT AFTERNOON SUN was getting low in the sky as shades of the short winter days were closing in on them. Mary murmured poetry over and over to herself, paying little attention to

anything. The girls sat quietly next to each other below deck with their backs up against the curved, wooden wall of the ship.

"Constance, do you have food enough to eat? Our once abundance is down to meager," Mary said, slowly shaking her head.

Constance broke off a piece of hard bread that she had been saving in her pocket and shared it with Mary.

Across the way Goodwife Hopkins was rocking her baby, being discreet as she opened her frock in front to nurse and quiet her wee one. For privacy she used a small handwoven coverlet to close out the noise and to gently cover his face and her own breast for modesty. With a candle glowing from their lantern, the girls examined the bread closely, hunting for any weevils.

"Our citrus is spoiled, and Mother is worried that we will come down with scurvy.[55] She says 'tis a most dreaded illness that haunts sea vessels," Mary said.

"Traveling by ship has changed the good breeding of people. Some take what is not theirs. The last of our good lemons were taken by somebody," Constance sadly answered.

The girls talked about what their mothers had taught them, each trying to sound like their mother.

"Never sit ye down at the table till asked and after the blessing."

"Ask for nothing, tarry till it be offered thee."

"Speak not."

"Bite not thy bread, but break it."

"Take salt only with a clean knife."

"Dip not the meat in the same."

"Look not earnestly at any other that is eating."

"When moderately satisfied, leave the table."

"Sing not, hum not, wriggle not."

The girls began to giggle.

Constance added, "All of these rules have been completely abandoned here."

"I have not seen it," Mary said, "but Johnny told me Master Allerton uses an iron implement[56] called a fork, brought from England. It has two sharp points to poke into food, kind of like a garden tool when pitching hay, but smaller!"

Mary shrugged her shoulders, "I just use my fingers and lick

---

[55] **Scurvy**: a disease resulting from a deficiency in vitamin C found in fruits such as oranges, lemons, and limes

[56] **Implement**: tool or instrument

them cleanly. Mother says indeed 'tis a vain thing to need an iron tool to hold on to her meat or any food!"

Mary tried her best again to mimic her mother's serious tone. "Our mothers worry that it will bring shame upon them."

The girls laughed.

Mary added, "Forgive me for saying so, but I saw Master Billington fumbling for an old, dried morsel of food in his bushy beard and enjoying every tidbit."

The two laughed and laughed.

"Truly," Mary went on in fun. "Imagine, a shred of hawk just dangling there for the taking."

They laughed again. It helped them forget their aching stomachs.

"Mother insisted on my learning this poem. It contains many wholesome rules for behaviors," Mary said as she cleared her throat, trying to sound grown up again. She began,

> When the meat is taken quite away,
> And voiders in your presence laid,
> Put you your trencher [57] in the same
> And all the crumbs which you have made.
> Take you with your napkin and knife,
> The crumbs what are before thee;
> In the voider a napkin leave . . . For it is courtesy.

"Hmm, haven't seen a napkin since London. I fear that soon

---

[57] **Trencher:** wooden platter for meat

we shall not even have crumbs to put on our trencher," Constance said, changing the mood.

"'Tis true," Mary said. "I heard Father and Master Brewster talking one evening in so serious a strain that we might suffer for enough food. Each person should be given a certain amount less than the appetite craves. It is a matter which cannot be helped."

"To think how excited I was when we first boarded this ship. I thought it was cozy with all the nooks and crannies," Constance admitted and continued with her head down. "Me Mum said these deplorable conditions are the hardest she has ever known. Me father says we have been at sea forty-three days and each day brings us several knots closer to the New World," Constance said. She hugged her knees as if trying to reassure herself.

"My father will have a fine tailor shop in the new colony," Mary said. "He is an expert tailor and pays attention to great detail. In Leyden, he would work patiently for hours, creating articles of clothing, making waistcoats, cloaks, and once, a stout pair of garters and breeches. His reputation was far and wide, but most of his patrons were poor. Some of his customers could not pay at all, so I am wearing one of the coats. 'Tis an old one and much mended, but it keeps me warm. He brought fine woolens with him and will do well in the new colony. After this voyage, don't ye think people will be in need of new clothing?"

Mary had confidence that her father would be very successful and it would allow them to send for the rest of their family in Green Gate. In her mind she could see their family settled in a sturdy cottage with a garden providing plenty for them and their neighbors too.

"Aye, and me father will be a grand tavern keeper in a fine inn, where he will serve food worthy of eating, not like the biscuits and moldy cheese that we eat day after day," Constance added with pride.

Out of nowhere the girls heard a gruff, reprehending voice. "Make known, ye Billington boys, if ye miss yer aim, ye'll mind yer mess!"

The ship was awash in foul odors, and lemon balm no longer helped the constant odor of the chamber pots.[58]

Mary sighed deeply. "Enough dreaming. 'Tis too dark down here to see or work our needles. I'm not accustomed to doing naught;[59] 'tis a shameful way to live. Constance, let's go have some merriment! Besides, those Billingtons are in trouble again, and they're heading up to empty the pot! Quick, let's move up first, away from them."

Mary couldn't stand the foul stench that came from the holds no matter which way the wind blew. The ship stank to the heavens! Captain Jones didn't mind the passengers on the top deck in fair weather and especially to carry out necessary duties and chores.

The girls peeked out of the crude wooden hatch door that led out to the upper deck.

"It has been days since I have seen a bit of sunlight. Come on, Constance, let's climb up!"

For a limited amount of time, the passengers were given permission to stretch on deck and enjoy fresh air and sunlight.

Despite the early murky dawn, the morning was clear and

---

[58] **Chamber pot:** A pot kept near the bed for nighttime bathroom use
[59] **"Doing naught":** doing nothing

sunny. The sun was now high enough to send dawn rays of light filtering down through the clouds and below, and water splashed against the side of the ship, causing gentle creaking of the timbers.

The ship's crew actually believed the rhyme:

"Red sky at night, sailor's delight.

Red sky in morning, sailors take warning.

If the sun rises red, the next day will be hot.

If it sets red, it will not."

Mary whispered, "The sailors have funny notions. I've been paying heed that the wintery sun has hung red and low on the horizon. Do you think what they say is true? With all of the cold storms, maybe 'tis so."

Mary's father joined them and said, "We have fresh, steady gales[60] with northeasterly winds. Take in a whiff of air. Some deep breaths are good for all of us!"

With excitement in her voice, Mary said, "Oh, look how the white canvas is catching the wind." One of her knit socks slid halfway down her leg. She quickly stretched it back up over her knee, all the while pointing and talking. "Look, the *Mayflower* is like a giant bird with all the sails swelling and flying against the wind!"

"Go up on deck now and get fresh air and make yourselves strong again! Move to the rail and make room," were the orders of Captain Myles Standish, an English military officer hired by the Pilgrims.

He summoned the men to straighten their backs and move smartly about the deck.

"Not yet, my young friend; it's not as easy as it looks." Officer Standish, had been working with the boys, showing them their weapons with serious concern.

The boys had joined the men topside to practice their skills

---

[60] **Gale**: a burst of strong wind

with firearms. Captain Standish worried about their lack of skill and set about to drill them hour after hour. The boys found it to be great sport, while Myles Standish wanted to ensure military defense and strict discipline. When they arrived in their new home, they had to be prepared for anything.

Mary and Constance watched the training for a while before getting distracted by the sailors up in the rigging.

"See the ratlines?" Mary's father pointed. "They are like rope ladders. The sailors climb hand over hand to the topsail yard. Then comes the worst part of all. See how they have to swing out onto the footropes to start adjusting the sails? There is nothing between them and death but air, a few ropes, and howling wind."

Mary was transfixed. What must it feel like to defy gravity, so high above ship and sea? A few of the seamen looked no older than her and Constance.

"They must be ready to do it in blizzards and rain and often in the pitch-black of the night. They hold on for dear life, yet try to work at the same time, high above the deck of this wildly pitching ship. They could be flung from the rigging into the deep at any moment!"

Constance, completely mystified, said, "Do you see? That's why I keep all those sailors in my prayers."

"I suppose ye are right, even though they mimic us with their gravelly voices," Mary said, trying to find some compassion. It wasn't easy. She was still miffed at one gruff old seaman in particular who seemed to delight in mocking them. At that very moment, Mary spied the old seaman frightening the daylights out of some of the youngest children.

He was telling them he'd throw them to the monsters in the sea, and he laughed as the little ones fled shrieking and crying to their mothers.

From the corner of her eye Mary saw his shipmates move

quietly back into the depths of the doorway, out of sight. She was filled with a fierce sense of injustice. How dare he try to frighten the little ones, and even worse, take pleasure in it? The blood rushed into Mary's head, and her heart hammered in her chest, but she was filled with a sudden fearlessness. Taking a step back, she looked at him with dislike in her eyes but did not flinch one bit. With all her gumption she boldly met his eyes and spoke right up to the crewman, who had no feelings and used language unfit for human ears. He fixed Mary with eyes narrowed to slits and a hairy smile that revealed his rotten teeth, and then threw a bushy-eyed glance at his fellow crewmen. But Mary was deliberate, leaning forward, clearing her throat, and gesturing heavenward with her hand.

"Be ye warned and take proper precaution. Moses of old parted the Red Sea for God's chosen children, and they were solely delivered safely to dry land!"

"Ye little snip," he spat.

Another sailor had to dive in front of him to stop him from grabbing her neck. Her heart nearly pounded out of her chest. Master Chilton, who had briefly walked away, only heard part of what was going on, but he quickly stepped forward, put a protective arm around Mary, and promptly led her down below.

"'Tis time to be on your guard, Mary. The seamen are becoming more aggressive and more agitated."

Still angry at the cruel sailor, Mary made bold[61] to her father and spoke up, putting her hands on her hips defiantly. "I am not afraid of that fearsome ogre."[62]

But at the same time she was trembling and half terrified.

"Mary, look at me," her father said firmly. "He is not to be outwitted!"

---

[61] **"Make bold"**: to act unafraid, confident, or abrupt
[62] **Ogre:** a hideous cruel man

Under her breath, she fumed, "I'll jolly soon see about that!"

"Listen to me." Her father held her firmly by her shoulders. "Things of importance are missing. You are to be on your guard. Valuables such as your gold locket are mysteriously disappearing, not to mention the physical danger that you can suffer. Look at me and promise me that you will stay clear of those sailors."

Mary could see in her father's eyes that he meant every word. Solemnly she simmered down and felt remorseful, promising to listen to what he bid. Out of habit she felt for her locket.

No one shall ever take my locket, she told herself.

That night she lay in her hammock, watching the lanterns cast wavering shadows on either side of the 'tween deck. After so much open air and excitement, Mary felt safe in the corner next to her mother and slept soundly. No amount of shaking could rouse her out of her sleep the next morning. When she finally woke up from her deep slumber, it was to astonishing news.

That very proud and most vulgar sailor who laughed every time someone vomited over the railing was dead! He had taken ill in the night and began to cast blood, dying shortly after. The crew had already taken his body topside, wrapped in canvas, and slid him over the rail. An odd thing it was, and the strange news shocked everyone and left them speechless.

"Imagine, Mary!" Constance said, shaking her head, "When someone else has misfortune, we mustn't take pleasure."

Mary wondered that the very man who threatened to throw half of the Pilgrims overboard was in fact the first to go. Because of superstitions among the sailors, their eyes got big and their heads hung low, and while they were still far from friendly to the Pilgrims, many of the worst insults stopped.

Just as a storm began to hit, Captain Jones learned of another problem. The Billington boys had tried to drown the ship's cat in a barrel of water.

"What is the meaning of this gross outrage? I demand an instant explanation!" he yelled.

John and Francis told a falsehood, claiming that they were trying to give it a bath.

The captain's hair rose as he exploded. "I'm on to ye two!"

He knew they were lying; you could see it in the set of his jaw. He gave them a good whipping as best he could, but both pulled lose and ran off. John, being the older of the two scoundrels, snuck around and kept to the captain's side like in a shadow. The ruckus was loud enough to wake the dead!

A sailor shouted, "I'll tan their hides," as he spit angrily into the wind. His voice sizzled like a hot poker plunged into water.

"That cat is worth the two of them. If we don't have a good cat aboard this ship, the rats will take it over. Not to mention a barrel of perfectly good water made putrid has now been wasted. They're enough to give the devil himself fits!"

Mary decided to stay as far away from the Billington boys as possible, but on such a small ship, she met up with them more often than she cared. John's sullen looks made her uncomfortable, but she was so naturally polite that she would always bob her head and murmur good day if they passed each other. Francis was more of a problem. He seemed to enjoy taunting her, and although Mary became adept at giving the younger of the Billington boys a wide berth, she feared it was only a matter of time before her luck ran out.

Chapter 11
The Unexpected

ON THE HIGH SEAS, the weather could change in the blink
of an eye. Out of nowhere, one mountainous wave crashed into the
ship, and for an awful moment or two it seemed she was bound
straight for the bottom of the sea. The ship was viciously shaken.
Some upper decks were very leaky as water poured into the cabins
from the open grated hatch. The ship pitched and tossed them
about wildly, and the Pilgrims became violently seasick. The
helmsman[63] was forced to lash himself to the wheel so he wouldn't
be washed overboard. Water swept across the decks while some of

---

[63] **Helmsman:** one who steers a ship

the swells[64] covered the tops of the masts. A crashing torrent of salt water broke through onto the passengers. Only God Himself knew exactly where they were . . . a little ship alone in this vast sea!

Below, they had never felt such fear. The ship pitched and rolled, and they were flung back against the timbers. A terrifying, loud snapping noise startled everyone. Mary had never heard such a terrible sound.

"Hurry . . . no time to waste!" Shouts came from every direction with thuds and pounding of feet overhead. The hatch was suddenly ripped open and Captain Jones leaned in.

"It's the beam! The main beam!" He yelled orders over the roar of the ocean, turned his back, and disappeared from view.

The crew followed, stooping as they went below. They raced down the ladder and pushed aside anything in their way. A random sea chest went sliding across the deck, just missing two small, whimpering children. The seamen didn't care who was in their way.

"Enough of your Psalm-singing and prayin'!"

The confusion and panic on board brought forth cries and screams. Some could hardly breathe, the fear was so intense.

"It's the timber that supports the main mast. It has split apart!" a seaman cried frantically.

"Hurry! Hurry!"

Frightened, Mary wondered if the *Mayflower* would sink. What was that small boat that Captain Jones had shown her? The shallop?

"Constance, what do you think? How many people do you think could fit into that shallop boat?"

"No more than twenty, I'm certain."

"If we have to leave this vessel, I mean, if we are really forced to abandon it, how long could we stay afloat?" Mary could feel her

---

[64] **Swell:** a wave, especially when long and unbroken, or a series of such waves.

heart racing. As the fearful moments closed in around them, she clung to her locket with full confidence that only God himself could save them, with His comfort and eternal security. She whispered a silent prayer.

Constance was alarmed. "Mary, surely there's no hope for our salvation in that shallop!"

Much as she wanted to be brave, Mary was completely paralyzed with fear. One glance at her friend told Mary that she was even more terrified. Mary took Constance's hand and found a small measure of peace in reassuring someone even more scared than she was.

Mary's father, though not well, joined in offering what strength he had. He wrapped one arm around his wife and the other around Mary. In spite of her father's presence, Mary's imagination went wild as she thought of these good people being washed away from the ship that must soon break into hundreds of pieces. She stopped such horrible thoughts as she felt a shiver go through her bones. With her head down and one hand covering her eyes, she desperately wished for something to hope for.

A plan was offered by some of the men from the Leyden group.

"An iron screw . . . a great iron screw was brought aboard this ship to be used in building a church in the New World. Let's use the screw," they quickly offered.

At first the seamen had too much pride to even consider the Pilgrims' idea. John Alden and others liked the idea, and after the ship's officers surveyed the damage below, they realized that they had no choice. Captain Jones had the last word and accepted their offer. He was mortally afraid that the end had come for his worthy ship.

"Maybe the *Mayflower* has sailed her last voyage," Captain Jones said. "We need something strong now to brace up the broken beam. Where is that great screw? Where is it stored? Someone tell us!"

No one, not even one man, could remember where the long screw had been placed. It had been packed away so well—not to be used until they landed in the New World.

"Where is that bloody screw?" Captain Jones shouted.

Panic and hopelessness filled the 'tween deck. Cracking and moaning sounds sent a new wave of stress and fear, until Master Chilton recalled seeing the huge screw.

"'Tis in the hold!" he called and motioned at the same time as best he could over the sound of the roaring ocean.

"Where I stored my trunk of woolen fabric. The screw is below in the hold next to me family's large trunk!" he shouted.

"To the hold we go!" yelled Captain Jones.

Desperately, they scrambled to the depths of the ship. Every minute counted. It took four men to carry the giant iron screw. Holding on for dear life, they braced themselves, and with all their muscular power and strength together, they heaved and pushed and maneuvered it directly under the broken beam and finally stabilized the massive timber.

"The mighty *Mayflower* is once again seaworthy![65] We can only hope it will hold," came the cries.

To the passengers on the 'tween deck, Captain Jones declared, "We are all safe now and beholden and grateful to Master James Chilton."

"Thanks to the quick mind of Master Chilton, we will move forward without fear. Now that the beam has been mended and the storm diminished, straight ahead is the New World, and by the grace of God and your prayers, we will arrive at our destination!"

"Thanks be to God," Mary's father said out loud with a huge sigh.

---

[65] **Seaworthy:** able to withstand stormy weather in safety; fit for a sea voyage

"Well done, Master Chilton, well done!" Cheers of relief filled the lower passageway.

Mary hugged her father and melted in his arms as the captain's voice rang in her ears. Her father was her hero, and she realized he had saved them by recalling where the giant screw was. No one else in all the excitement had the presence of mind to know what to do.

The storm passed, taking one danger with it, but there were other things to fear. Mary had heard Captain Jones explaining to her father that ships always traveled in twos and threes for safety's sake, especially to be protected from pirates. Each ship was painted with their own bright colors, so seamen could identify the ships by sight. Nerves were a trifle on edge. The loss of the *Speedwell* as a companion had made this voyage more vulnerable because of the hazard of a single ship traveling alone on the high seas with the burden of extra passengers, many more than had been planned.

Rounding a corner at the opposite end of the 'tween deck, Mary blinked with surprise to see Johnny standing inside one of John Alden's barrels.

"Oh, there ye are, Mary," John Alden called out. He held out a pair of well-worn britches.

Johnny spoke up, "Them're mine, Mary. Would ye, could ye, please stitch 'em up for me?"

Pointing, he said, "'Tis me bottom part and knee, needs a new patch."

Mary tried not to laugh too much at the sight of Johnny, all pink and cold and covered with goose bumps, stuck in a barrel.

"I will do what I can, but they look fairly threadbare." She donned an impish smile and said, "Don't ye go very far, Johnny!"

He waited and waited in that empty barrel while Mary took extra care using the blue thread that was already in her needle.

'Twas a good thing, she thought, because it was difficult to thread a needle on a swaying ship with little or no light. She used a scrap of wool from an old coverlet to patch on top of the worn-out patches. She knew Johnny was not going anywhere, so she took a few extra minutes and embroidered a small emblem. Then, her needle in and out, she made a final knot.

As she folded up the mended britches, she thought to herself, "Would I ever dare to wear britches?"

She shook them out again and held them up and thought they would certainly be more sensible on a ship than all these heavy skirts and petticoats.

She sent them back with little Joseph. "Be swift and take these to Johnny Hooke. Don't tarry along the way. He stands shivering and waiting in a barrel!"

It took a few days before Johnny noticed the small, embroidered heart in the corner of his patch. He grinned from ear to ear. From that day on, every time he looked at his left knee, he thought of Mary.

One afternoon, when the sea was less angry and the wind was steady, several of the children were allowed on the main deck to take in some sun and fresh air. Constance was down below, rocking Oceanus to sleep, so Mary visited with the four More children. The oldest was Elinor. Only a few years younger than Mary, she seemed old beyond her years. Jasper and Richard were just a few years behind her in age. They were brown haired and freckled, but far too serious for lads of eight and seven. The baby of the family was the little girl who had snuggled so close during Mary's stories.

"How came ye to be traveling to the New World?" Mary asked. There was silence before Richard blurted out, "Me father does nay want us no more."

"Oh, Richard." Mary was dismayed. What could she say? She looked questioningly at Elinor, unable to believe such an awful thing.

Elinor nodded solemnly and said, "'Tis true. He has torn us from our mother's arms, and sent us ever so far away. I fear we will never again see her." Little Mary's tears overflowed at her sister's bleak words and she hid her face in Elinor's apron. Jasper pressed his lips firmly together as if he were trying to be manly and not cry, but Mary could see a shadow in his eyes as well.

A scripture came to Mary's mind, something her father had read once in their little windmill with a cheerful fire blazing and her family gathered safe around while he read from the Bible. Now she shared it. "Many waters cannot quench love, neither can the floods drown it." She was pleased to see a small smile on Elinor's face, and little Mary gave a final sniff and lifted her head. Jasper's eyes lit up hopefully.

Richard lifted his chin and stated, "When I am grown, I will build me own ship and sail back for Mother, and I will bring her back to us."

Jasper, not to be outdone by his younger brother, piped up. "Aye, and I will build her a house, and we will be together once more."

Now Mary felt her own tears welling up. Leaving Leyden and her loved ones behind had been so hard. Sometimes she had felt so alone, but now she realized that everyone had their own burdens to bear. Her own seemed very small compared to the Mores' heartbreak. And yet, they were so brave. Right then and there, Mary decided she would try to always be as courageous as her new friends.

Over the next several days, the winter turned. With the shifting darkness of the sea, temperatures fell drastically as the wind rose with an ice storm that thrashed against the sides of the ship. Many passengers were still too weak to leave their beds, including Mary's father. There were many trips above deck to empty buckets over the side. There was need of fresh water to soak rags and wipe faces.

"Mum, I'm cold, on the verge of freezing. I can't remember when I was last warm." Mary turned to her mother with her lips quivering. "If only I could have an hour of sunshine, that is all I would ever ask for."

The fair weather had long vanished for good. The sea was unrelenting as it continued rising, becoming more of a threat each day. There could be no cooking fires, and candles were completely snuffed for fear of fire.

"Oh, my hands are numb and stiff. I can't feel them."

"Here, let me take your hands," her mother gently offered. "I will rub them until they are warm again."

Her mother's fingers felt rigid and chilled, but the ache and cold were diminished by her comforting touch.

"Trials are tests of our faith," Mother whispered, giving her daughter a tender look. Many times Mary recalled her mother saying, "Face the sunshine and let the shadows fall behind." That was easy to do when the sun was shining. But now the sunshine was fading, leaving dull, gray shadows. Mary thought of the Mores and pushed the negative thoughts away. Mary's shaky smile seemed to strengthen her mother, for she added, "We are stronger today because of all we have endured and will continue to endure." For a moment, their fears were eased.

Mary said, "I could have much more faith and love of the Lord if I didn't have bugs in me gruel."

"Mary, 'tis blasphemous to measure faith and love of God to mere bugs!" said her mother.

Just then, as if John and Francis Billington knew how Mary felt, they called out, "Hey there, Mary Chilton, look here," as they popped one, two, three bugs into their mouths!

"We just had a fresh bug pie, we did. Here, catch yers."

And they threw a dead bug at Mary.

"Oh, ye awful boys, go away!"

In disgust, Mary shook the bug from her hair onto her skirt, and flung it completely away.

"Shoo, ye nasty Billingtons!" someone called out.

The boys threw their heads back laughing and said, "Ye better get used to them bugs. Rations are wormy and all but gone!"

Mary's mother said peevishly, "Always a source of foolishness and pranks."

Later, Mary approached the galley where the women were cooking and eavesdropped. She heard snatches of conversation. "Winter . . . storms at sea . . . how will we plant in the colony in midwinter . . . winter in full force . . . how will we build a shelter?"

Soon, worries were expressed only in whispers. Mary knew sometimes situations were exaggerated and made worse or better than they really were. But now the women looked somber and grim-faced. No one was smiling.

Mary's mother spoke up with conviction. "We'll do our best, and angels can do no better."

Another added, "Aye, we shall cross that bridge when we come to it and in the meantime keep a stiff upper lip!"

That night, pleading, Mary asked, "Mum, when will we be there? How much longer do we have to stay in this dank, smelly ship? I miss my sisters." Homesickness swept over her. "Do ye miss our family in Leyden, Mum?"

"Oh, aye, Mary." Her hand lingered as she reached out and brushed it across Mary's cheek.

"Truly, will we ever see them again? How will they find us or even know where we will be?"

"Shh, dear one, we must trust in God. He will surely guide us all."

The voyage was taking longer than planned, and the spoiled rations for each family were cut again with no land in sight. Their clothes and coverings were constantly wet and cold. They reeked of mildew and became stiff when the salt water dried.

Normally, people bathed at least once a season, but since setting out from Leyden in June, there had been little opportunity for bathing. Vinegar, oils and herbs, even salt water were used to clean hair and skin.

Now that the winter storms were upon them, there was little chance to go on deck. The passengers were forced to keep the hatch closed to prevent more water from entering. Because they lived in near darkness, they even lost track of time. Through it all, Mary's mother was a pillar of strength, and that's why Mary was surprised to see her eyes brim with tears. When Goodwife Chilton became aware that Mary was watching her, she tried to hide them by looking away. "With the hunger and cold and sickness on every hand, it is as if we have been abandoned by our Maker," she said to herself, so softly that only Mary heard.

The voyage was etched on her tired, gaunt face. Mary decided at that moment not to tax her mother's heart further by complaining ever again.

The next day, when Constance was feeling sad and missed England, Mary shared with her how not to be homesick.

"You simply imagine things—you let yourself be in another place. For example, I recall every object in our windmill house. Every day I try to create a different memory of something, even count the timbers in the wall or trace the cracks in the plaster. I count the skeins of woolen yarn in Mum's basket on our windowsill. I step outside and see the houses far off in Leyden, the cobblestone streets and lane of Green Gate, and each dear face of me friends. Try it, Constance. It works. Those little thoughts will last forever."

During a lull in between storms, Mary and Constance finished their chores and climbed the stairs to push the heavy hatch door open. Squinting their eyes to adjust to the brightness of the overcast sky, they were in earshot of the sailors. The girls slipped through, staying away in the opposite direction. One sailor gave a mighty belch and the crew was paralyzed with laughter. They called each other inferior names, everything from "Gob" to "Seadog." One poor sailor who had a wooden peg leg was called "Hip-pity." He hopped around with one leg shorter than the other, trying to keep up with the younger ones. To the Pilgrim children, it was a wonderment how he lost his leg. Johnny Hooke insisted it was by a giant sea monster!

Keeping their distance from the sailors, the girls delighted in the brief bit of daylight. Leaning over the rail was one of the few rules that was not taken seriously and was almost always broken.

"Smell the air. Isn't it lovely and fresh?"

The air carried a sharp briny smell, but they were so used to it that they no longer paid attention. They stood aside as the sailors splashed the deck with seawater and vinegar.

"Wet them boards—it keeps 'em tight," an old seaman told a young sailor.

Salt spray filled the air as water pounded against the side of the ship. Mary knew it was kind of a daring thing to be on deck this close to the sailors, but the young sailors were nicer than the old ones, and the girls stayed clear. Trying to find reason to stay topside, they giggled and dared each other to do little things to pester the sailors. Perhaps they would pay dearly for this moment of fun.

"Go ring the bell; it signals the change of watches," urged Mary daringly.

"Oh no, I shan't."

"Watch me, Constance." Mary timed it just right. She tapped a "mate" on the shoulder and acted as though it wasn't her, skipping quickly ahead, scrunching up her shoulders, and glancing back at Constance with a mischievous grin. Constance stood there in total shock!

"Your turn, Constance. See the knit cap sitting there? Toss it over-board!"

To Mary's surprise, Constance impulsively grabbed it and gave it a good fling, but it hit the ropes and fell back on to the deck! They turned quickly so no one would see them giggling. In that moment the girls felt just a bit sinful and guilty, nudging each other in anticipation of being reprimanded. The sailors paid no attention. Mary had never within her memory, until now, been tempted to do anything that would bring shame on her parents or especially to disappoint God or bring His displeasure. She knew she would surely need to repent of their deeds.

The two friends enjoyed the new fresh feeling of being on the upper deck. Suddenly the sun was with them again. They peered down beyond the railing of the ship and enjoyed the breeze. Somewhere over the endless horizon was the New World, and this same breeze had blown over that land just recently. Surely they must arrive soon. If the wind could cross such long distances, so would they, until they safely landed.

Mary wiped her nose on her sleeve, and Constance licked her burned and parched lips and wrapped her arms around herself to keep warm. It was unusual to feel the warmth of the sun and they took these rare moments to get dry. Mary tried to push the flying strands of her wet hair from across her cheeks back neatly beneath her coif.

"My coif no longer keeps my hair clean." Mary's curly hair was matted and filthy.

Constance offered, "I use a pinch of lavender on my hair. It helps it to smell better."

"Oh, I am certain I will need more than just a pinch—more like a fistful to rub all over me head!"

They heard, "Starboard a little, full-and-by, steady now."

Sailors constantly worked to keep a ship seaworthy.

The sailors began to sing as they pulled the ropes made of hemp for the sails and swabbed the decks.

"Come all ye young fellows who follows the sea, to me way, hey, blow the man down."

Listening to the sea chanties was great entertainment for two Pilgrim girls. Their hair and clothes began to dry as the sunshine broke through the clouds. Sunlight filtered through the sail onto Mary's cinnamon colored ringlets at the nape of her neck, from beneath her coif. The girls swayed a little with the movement of the ship and Mary reached up with both arms outstretched. Could she possibly hold on to the last bit of warmth?

"My parents spent their last farthing, pound and pence, for us to come on this voyage."

"Mine did the same, Mary."

"Constance, God tells us to trust Him with our hearts. That true riches are friends and family that love ye and stand by ye."

"Aye, me mum says, real wealth comes from rewards for good works and deeds and by the grace of God."

"Mum tells me that as well," Mary said.

"Mary, I haven't told ye this . . . but me real mum died a few years ago. Me stepmum is Goodwife Hopkins."

Mary was flabbergasted for a brief moment. "I'm so sorry to hear that Constance . . . I thought she was yer real mum. She seems nice as if ye were her own daughter."

"Aye, 'tis a good chance I have such care from her."

"Is Master Hopkins your real father?"

"Aye, and a good one at that."

Just like she had with the More family, Mary realized that everyone had some difficulty, some adversity that they must overcome.

"I overheard Mistress Mullins tell someone that ye are the apple of your father's eye."

"I have heard." Mary sighed, rolling her eyes. "She fears that I am pampered because of being my parents' youngest child. For my own part, I cannot see how I do less reverence to my parents. Once in a while I do ask a question, but very politely, and they do not seem to mind giving me an answer. 'Tis the same with Captain Jones. In fact, he encourages me. Sometimes I just burst with questions I can't help meself, keeping half of them inside me. Constance, don't ye just want to know everything?"

"I suppose, but girls need to be content with home and hearth, children and gardens. That is me dream someday. Will we still be friends when we are eighteen like Priscilla Mullins? Or do we have to live a proper grownup's life? I wonder if our work will become our play or how everything will be then? We are almost women now!" Constance said.

"I don't know. While I think I'm almost thirteen years old, I've never really kept track and have never thought to ask. I don't even know what I look like," Mary replied, shrugging her shoulders. She had no real need to look at herself, either. Mary simply never bothered to know.

"Once I looked into a clear barrel of water. 'Tis how ye can see who ye really are," suggested Constance.

"I do know that my eyes are blue," Mary said with confidence. "And that my hair is a reddish color. And yours Constance, is a bonny golden glow of color." Mary's mother always taught her to never suppress a generous thought. "I'm so glad to have a friend like ye, Constance."

"Me as well. We'll have many jolly good times together." Constance gave a sigh, a double shiver, and a sneeze at the same time.

"Bless ye!"

The late afternoon warmth turned chill while evening set in, and the stars grew fuller and larger around them. A yellow moon appeared suddenly and silently to keep them company and listen to their talk. The *Mayflower* herself was bathed in moonlight.

"I've been thinking, Mary. Good times won't end when we become fourteen or fifteen years old," Constance said.

"That's true," Mary said. She was filled with excitement as she thought of what the future might hold for them. She threw her arms into the air enthusiastically. "There will be so much more for us to do in the new colony, and someday we'll have our own cottages and our own children."

In a more serious tone Mary said, "Someday, I want to tell my children about this voyage. I hope God gives me many children. Who will remember this time, this adventure, if we forget to tell our children?"

With hope in her voice, Constance asked, "Mary, what if the rest of your life was the best of your life?"

Mary tried to grasp what her future world would look like.

Now, Mary had thoughts that she had never had before. Some were troubling to her.

"Someday this will be a grand story to tell, but . . ."

"Is something wrong?" Constance asked.

"I don't know why I feel anxious," Mary said. "There is nothing sure on earth except the rising and setting of the sun and, when the sky is quilted over with black storm clouds and there is no line between earth and heaven, who could know where we are or what the sun is doing?

"We've been aboard the *Mayflower* for so long. What if we never see land again?" Mary continued.

The girls stood together at the railing and stared at the dark water streaked with the pale light of the moon and thought desperately about when they might see land again. They looked toward the west where they had hopes for a New World.

The sky changed from azure to dark, dull gray. Despite her sober thoughts, Mary savored the moment when the breeze picked up. Captain Jones had told her, "The more wind in her sails, the faster she will move." Mary longed to see just a sliver of land and was happy that the ship was cutting through the waves into the vast open sea toward their new home.

Just as Constance started down the stairs to get another coverlet and peer in on baby Oceanus, Johnny trudged up, looking very grim, but his expression brightened when he saw Mary.

"To what do I owe this pleasant surprise?"

Each had a big smile for the other.

"What brings ye topside, Johnny Hooke?" Mary inquired.

"Just dumped over a bucketful—not me favorite duty!"

Mary drew a shuddering breath. "That must be dreadful!" She could not imagine doing such a task as emptying the "pot" overboard like that.

"I don't fancy it, but 'tis better than being sent to the workhouse where orphans are forced to toil fourteen hours a day in filthy conditions. Here at sea I can see the sky, breathe in fresh air, and feel freedom just out there beyond the horizon."

He hesitated a bit before he continued. "Aye, 'tis true. In the drudgery of it all, we learn no trade. We are exploited[66] in order to eke out a mere living for scraps of nasty leftovers."

Mary was surprised to learn such troubling and sad things, things that Johnny seemed to know only too well.

"But now John Alden is teaching me how to make barrels and kegs so I can be a proper cooper one day."

Still thinking about what Johnny had just shared with her, but changing the subject, Mary asked, "John Alden? Is he the one I hear who is sweet on Priscilla Mullins?"

"Don't know much about that." Johnny sniffed and wiped his nose on his sleeve.

"John Alden is one of them grown-ups, and only grown-ups can ask all them questions." He continued good-naturedly, "Older folks can say, 'What's your name?' 'How old are ye?' 'Keep your nose clean.' If we ever turned the questions around the other way and said, 'Wash your face,' 'Take your hat off!' or 'My, how you've grown!'—we'd get a royal whack!"

Mary agreed with a laugh. In a more serious tone, she said, "I think every human has something to say or cry about, don't ye?"

"Aye, your father, Mary. I don't mind listenin' to what he has to say. He is a valiant man. Captain Jones is mighty pleased that he is aboard his ship. Sure and it would have gone down with all of us if it weren't for your resolute father. When that beam began to split, it scared me out of me skin!"

---

[66] **Exploited**: to use selfishly for one's own ends

Mary quickly added, "Aye, Father says by God's assistance we shall prevail."

"That sounds proper respectful," Johnny said. "He gained great marvel from me, he did!"

Mary wanted to know more about Johnny. "Did ye have many friends in Leyden, I mean, when ye are an orphan, can ye have friends?"

"Aye, 'tis a sad lot indeed to be deprived of happiness. From day to day, ye never know who ye trust or who's a proper friend. So when I say I have heaps of chums, that's not the way it truly is. I simply protect meself. That way no one asks too many questions. Them times are dark memories."

Without warning, the wind quickened, snapping the sails and giving the ship a mighty shake.

Johnny took Mary's hand. "We'd better quick get down below!"

Buckets of water fell from the sky. Canvas was flapping and wood creaking as though it was close to splitting. Johnny had barely opened the hatch in time and rushed Mary down the ladder when an enormous wave hit and they lost their balance. Falling and rolling among the casks,[67] they held on to each other as they acquired bruises and splinters. The thunderous violence of the storm broke all around them.

Johnny lost hold and reached out in the dark for her. "Mary I'm here. Take me hand."

"Where are ye? I can't see."

"I'm coming."

---

[67] **Cask:** A barrel-like container

He reached for her with all his strength and pulled her in close to him, protecting her from anything that might fall.

Mary was shaking and cold.

"Just stay here with me. I'll keep ye safe," Johnny said.

Mary waited for the giant sea to rush over them, but it didn't come. She lost all sense of time in the wet darkness below. The 'tween deck had its own small tides as the ship rocked back and forth. The terror of plunging and pitching through the vast sea caused Mary's heart to pound, and she held on tighter, glad to have the comfort of a friend.

The ship had plunged down into a trough between giant waves. They felt as though they were on the very point of being yanked out of the earth and carried heavenward all at the same time. Johnny smoothed her hair gently and tucked her curls into her coif, then kissed her gently on her forehead to calm her. The ship was still rolling from side to side when he lifted her to her feet, keeping his arms around her until she was steady again.

Looking into her eyes and holding her head in his hands, he said, "There, how are ye now?"

"That was an awful fright. I thank thee, Johnny. I don't know what I would have done without ye."

"Aye, ye were floating about and bumping into the lot of it! Take care of ye, I'll see ye soon." He reached up with a jump and touched a rope above his head, and said with a wink, "Well, I'd better go and get on with it, I'm  indentured[68] to Master Allerton, ye know, till I'm twenty-four years old. If he catches me here, I'm done fer."

---

[68] **Indentured:** to be a servant

He turned and leaped up to touch another rope, snatched up a bucket, and was on his way, taking three steps at a time.

Constance appeared just as Johnny was headed up topside and announced, "Through all of that, little Oceanus is well asleep!"

Tugging at Mary's skirt from behind, she chattered away. "That storm hit and left us just as fast as it came! Mary, are ye all right? That Johnny seems like a nice everyday chap." Mary could tell that Constance hoped she would say more.

Still a little pale, Mary said, "Aye, I think he is a most . . . well, a clever boy."

She was deep in her thoughts with Johnny's tale of woe and their terrifying experience of being tossed all around. Her face was warm with a blush. She felt her heart still racing a bit. Then she noticed her cheeks were stinging and cracked from the dry salt on her face, and she gave a shiver from being wet. Breathing in and out, she could see her breath in the cold air and could still feel Johnny's protective arms around her. She licked her lips to taste the salt on her mouth from the seawater.

The day had turned from sunny to stormy to gray, then to an indigo-blue night. By now, the rain began to fall again in sheets, with water blowing down onto their heads. The hatch had not been closed yet as the girls scrambled for cover as raindrops pelted them. They hurried and pulled the heavy hatch shut and made their way to their families. Mary settled in for the night, her last thoughts of feeling warm and safe in Johnny's arms.

Chapter 12
Will-O'-the-Wisp

THE DAY-TO-DAY VOYAGE WAS hard on Mary's father. Being the oldest of all the Pilgrims, he was unable to move around much and became weaker with each passing day. Mary whiled away the time dreaming about the day that they would see land. Hunger and thirst were becoming more and more familiar. Like their parents, the children wore the same clothes day after day, week after week, getting dirtier and more worn all the time. A smell of wet wool stuffed her nostrils. The air was thick and stagnant—it was no longer unusual to spot a mouse, or even a rat, or see bugs crawling around. By now the hardtack,[69] salted pork, and fish were gone. Everyone washed as best they could with the seawater. Splinters were always getting into little fingers and toes. Many of the Pilgrims fell to their knees, and in spite of suffering, gave thanks to be alive, while some of the shipmates wept openly.

"Be sparing with the water—we have precious little," was often heard.

The ship rolled from side to side for days on end, causing falls and spills. For safety and warmth, the passengers kept to their hammocks and bunks. Sleeping, for some, was a quiet escape. Lying

---

[69] **Hardtack:** unleavened bread, large wafers

there, nestled in her hammock, Mary peered over the edge, listening to the sound of footsteps overhead on the main deck. Hearing the long, continuous drone, she slipped easily into slumber, even with the sounds of a hundred others around her. Within minutes she fell quietly into a dreamy slumber . . .

Mary's eyes adjusted from the brilliant sunshine outside as she entered the darkness of a petite cottage. She could barely make out the shape of a single cloak hanging on a wooden peg. She entered the small doorway to a cozy room. There were two windows with a fireplace between them. The flames in the hearth flickered and danced before her eyes. Rough stone walls were whitewashed with wattle and daub—a mix of straw, animal hair, lime, and mud plaster. She could see bits of straw in the mud between the timber beams in the low ceiling that stretched across to the top of the windows. Through blurred glass, Mary could see a small graveyard and a field of lavender beyond that—it looked like a coverlet of purple linen.

She pulled herself from the warmth of the fire as her father suddenly appeared and beckoned her outside, down a random pathway, and through a rusty garden gate. It screeched as he pushed it open.

"Come, Mary." Her father took her by the hand.

"Now turn around," he said quietly.

Her eyes traveled from a thatched roof made of marsh reeds and hay to the circling smoke that came from the chimney, then down to the miniature cottage, and finally, her eyes settled below on the humble headstones. She was focused on every detail. Years of wind and harsh weather had all but removed the carved names from the faded headstones. Green moss, soft and velvety to the touch, covered the stones, and the mayflower bushes were blushing with creamy pink blossoms. The winter covering of old leaves crunched underfoot.

"Some of the gravestones are so tiny," Mary said.

Tufts of grass almost hid some of them from sight.

Father spoke. "Your grandmother Isabelle lives here. She built this cottage with her bare hands and chops firewood and tends to her garden. If this modest cottage could speak, it would tell us a thousand things. My father was ill, and they had very little to live on. Grandmother Isabelle grew beans, root vegetables, and herbs, and produced her own cheese and butter and wool. I am the only child that survived. Nana buried four of her little ones right here. Throughout her life she managed to remain steadfast and undaunted by affliction. With every reason in the world to give up, she never did. Ye have that same unwavering blood running through your veins, Mary."

Mary's dream continued on as her father showed her more and told valiant stories of her fearless grandmother.

Just as Mary felt overwhelmed, her father suddenly exclaimed, "Look, a candle glows in the window. There is movement in the cottage, and I can see the likes of Nana moving about."

Mary felt chills go all through her, and with both arms she clung to her father as they seemed to float through the air and through the thick walls of the cottage. There before them stood a petite, pleasant woman with an apple face and dimples in her cheeks. Her eyes were sparkling blue, and her arms reached out to embrace Mary. From the corner of her eye, her father slowly vanished.

"My sweet Mary, how I've missed thee." Mary didn't think it strange that her grandmother had missed her. Mary felt the same, even though they had never met. It was like being with a dear friend that one hadn't seen for ages.

Together with her grandmother, she danced, twirling across the cozy teapot-sized room. Such joy and sweet companionship Mary had never known before. They talked for hours or years—time held no meaning here. But then there was a subtle shift in the room, and a radiant light gathered around her grandmother. Nana cupped Mary's face in her hands and spoke. "Our special time together is drawing to a close, child. I pray that the Comforter will be with thee. Before we are parted, I would tell thee something of great import. Then she leaned forward and whispered into

Mary's ear, fading away into the light as she did so, until Mary was left alone in the afterglow.

Mary slowly woke and realized that her dream of the faraway cottage was vanishing. What was real, and what was a dream? Both were blending together yet fading away. Curled up in her hammock, she felt sad that it had all been a dream. It had felt so real. Snuggling deep into her covers and lumpy clothes, she closed her eyes tight. Maybe if she concentrated with all her might, just maybe she could bring back her remarkable dream. The more she tried to get back into her dream, the more awake she became. Finally, she got up and slipped over to her mother's side, gently shaking her shoulder.

"Mum, I was in a dream—yet did not sleep. It was more than a dream!"

Every detail of her vision-like dream was sharp and clear.

"I saw Nana, and she spoke to me in Old English!"

Mary had never been so anxious to share her feelings with her mother before. With her wise mother's full attention, Mary recited her grandmother's words:

Woulds't thou seeth the truth and be free?
Then sound and honest thou must choose to be.
Do not be quick to judge with brevity,[70]
The highest wisdom comes from adversity.
If thou wilt be diligent and gather wheat,
The binding labour will thus taste sweet.

Her mother was astonished!

---

[70] **Brevity:** to be brief

"Mary, this makes my hair stand on end. Ye may think it strange to hear me speak thus, but 'tis the very way Nana spoke, in a manner of old English. The very description of her . . . the very likeness of her cottage. Father must hear every word, every last shred of your dream! Go, child, in haste to tell him. Do not tarry."

Mary made her way in the darkness, barefoot through the early morning shadows. She crept across bedding and over coverlets. Men snored and mumbled in their sleep as she tried to adjust her steps. She caught her foot in a coil of heavy rope and fell forward.

"Whoa!" came a cry.

The odor of unwashed bodies and clothes was overwhelming.

A man's full voice boomed, "What do ye want, a woman at this end of the deck?"

"Me father," she whispered timidly. "Master Chilton, do ye know where he lies?"

"Over there," a dark shadow said with a scowl. In a whisper, Mary said, "Thank ye" and hurried to her father's side.

"Father, 'tis me, Mary."

He responded slowly. "My child, what is the hurry?"

As Mary retold her father the dream, her eyes blurred with tears and she sat in wonderment beside her father. His eyes also shone with tears.

When she was finished, he took her in his arms and simply said, "Mary, ye have met your Grandmother Isabelle!"

Chapter 13
A Broad Sweep of Events

SHAKING OUT THE LINEN and coverlets topside was a good opportunity to get some fresh air.

"Lay hold of it, Constance," Mary hollered. "Take the corners, get a tight grip, now shake hard!"

The heavy coverlets made of woolen patches kept slipping out of Constance's hands. The girls laughed and tried again. "One, two, three—shake!" Today the sun was trying to make its way through the thick, gray clouds, and the deck was crowded with passengers hungry to escape the dark, dank innards of the ship. Unfortunately, this day Francis Billington was one of them. Lately, he wanted Mary's attention and did mean, nasty things whenever he could get away with it.

He would shout things like, "Mary keeps her nose in the air" or, "What good are yer prayers doin'? God don't hear 'em!"

Anything to turn her head, anything, and he tried it. Mary always stayed her distance and refused to pay him and his little schemes any attention.

Both of the girls were so busy in their task that neither of them noticed Francis Billington peeking up through the open hatch. Without warning, he sprang up and grabbed Mary's ankle.

"Now I got you," he growled, pulling her.

Mary let out a scream. The coverlet went flying out of her hands and struck Constance, sending her against the railing.

"Let me go!" Mary yelled. Losing her balance, Mary stumbled backward right on top of Francis's head, and the two of them fell.

Johnny Hooke, standing below, saw it all happen as Mary lost her footing. Before he could move, the two tumbled, crashing down the ladder headfirst and barely missing the "bucketful" that Johnny was about to empty. Quickly, Johnny jumped aside as they hit the hard 'tween deck floor. Mary had banged her head a good one and was crying and dazed. Francis gave an irritating laugh, acting as if he wasn't hurt and it had all been in jest.

Looking down the ladder, Constance cried, "Oh my, Mary, are ye all right down there?"

Rubbing her shoulder, Constance bunched up the bedding, not exactly sure yet what had happened, for the coverlet had blocked her view. Johnny had seen it all and was furious. He grabbed ahold of Francis before he could get away, pulling him up by his britches and shoving him up against the hard wall of the ship.

"Ye have the brains of a pea, ye do! Sooner or later . . ."

"Ah, yer talking a light bit of rubbish," snapped Francis.

"I have half a mind to throw ye in the drink! Keep your grubby hands off Mary, you hear?"

With a smirk, Francis cleared his throat and spit right into Johnny's face. That was all the encouragement Johnny needed. His strength seemed suddenly to double as he tightened his grip with one hand and with the other doubled up his fist and slugged Francis right in the nose.

"Yah dirty dolt,[71] go now and cry to yer ma!"

---

[71] **Dolt:** a stupid person

"Ahhh! He hit me," Francis whimpered out loud. His nose was bleeding as he ran off looking for sympathy.

Johnny turned to reach for Mary, who was on one elbow straightening her skirts and struggling to get up. She was still dizzy from the blow to her head. For the first time, she was glad to be wearing all of her frocks at once. They had cushioned her fall.

"I'll clobber that mindless imbecile[72] if he ever comes near ye again, Mary. I promise. Are ye feeling well enough now? Ye are very pale." He wiped her eyes and nose with his shirt tail. "Sorry, 'tis not too clean."

Mary didn't care. Constance scrambled down the ladder and wrapped her shawl around Mary. "One minute ye were topside, and the next ye were gone out of sight!"

Usually Mary felt hardy and unafraid of anything, especially those dreaded Billingtons. But this time, Francis had taken her off guard and frightened her good, and now she was sputtering and angry. Johnny stayed by her side till her nerves had recovered and then helped her up to her feet as she wiped her tears away with the back of her hand. Johnny had a way of making her feel safe and protected.

She straightened her coif. "It is impossible to say quite all that ye feel when your head is so full of anxious thoughts!"

From now on, she knew that if the Billington boys ever tried anything, Johnny would come to her rescue and put them in their place, with everyone's blessing. Mary chose not to share this dreadful incident with her parents. She knew it would be too upsetting.

Lately, Mary was always hungry. She felt such a violent pang of

---

[72] **Imbecile:** fool, mindless

hunger that she pushed her fist against her stomach to take away the ache. Her eyes held fast to the horizon, her mind lost in thought as she glanced over the vast sea a hundred shades of blue. They made her think of Remy, far away in Leyden, and how he would have noticed the many changing colors of the ocean.

It was almost sunset, an end to another long day. She stretched her arms up to the moon as thick swirls of fog began to roll in. Then with a sudden chill, she wrapped her arms around herself tight. Mary worried about her parents and what their future would hold. All night long there was constant coughing. Nearly everyone was sick and sprawled all over the 'tween deck below. The ship was cramped and dank. The hours ran on endlessly as the ocean continued to swell, causing the vessel to pitch and yaw. Through the night, little children fretted and whined.

They weren't the only ones. The sailors were grumbling and found the Pilgrims more bothersome. Heavyhearted, the Pilgrim Fathers experienced grave concern over the growing mistrust and division between the sailors and the passengers.

Groups of the pilgrims gathered, speaking in hushed voices. One old man sagely commented, "They seem to be vexed that we may not land near Virginia, where we had planned. We are much farther north and far out of jurisdiction. Some of the passengers feel that since we are not near the designated area, they are not bound to obey and be governed by our grant and its rules that we all agreed to. How do we feel about this?"

Master Mullins threw a bushy-eyed glance and added, "Some have openly refused to work for the company and contribute in any way toward repayment for the voyage. They want to strike out on their own and keep the fruits of their labors for themselves."

Master Hopkins said with alarm and disbelief, "This would place an unbearable debt on the rest of us! It could mean placing power in the hands of those least able to make sensible decisions, leaving lawless cabbage heads to govern this venture!"

Mary found Constance and confided, "I overheard folks talking of trouble on the ship. Little groups here and there are knotted together, casting dark looks over their shoulders at one another and at the leaders. Some do not want to honor their promise to uphold the rules they agreed upon."

"Why would they do that?" Constance wondered.

"I think they are selfish," Mary tried to keep her voice down. "They only want to help themselves and not the colony." She softened her voice even more, "I heard Father saying a mutiny could be close at hand—and 'tis spreading all over the ship!"

"Mutiny? Why, that's terrible."

"Aye, Constance, 'tis not good at all when nobody follows the rules and there's no order. Worst of all, those awful sailors would take command of the ship."

"They'd take the ship? But Captain Jones would never allow that to happen," Constance said.

"Find courage, Constance. They would grab him and tie him up!" In her excitement, Mary realized their voices had risen, and she dropped back to a whisper. "Shhh, nobody should hear this."

Constance's eyes widened and Mary's heart felt like it was in her throat as she realized what she had just said. She looked around, desperate to know what was going on and equally desperate not to appear to be listening in on the grown-ups, who were keeping it quiet among themselves.

"Oh, Constance, there is more. You must hide your Bible! I put ours under my pillow." With her hands cupped to her mouth, she whispered, "The Rogers family Bible was slashed into several bits with a knife when no one was around."

"Mary, I pray God forgive them. I fear for us."

"There is no trust. We must be prudent," Mary warned. "The sailors believe all sorts of peculiar superstitions. They are mostly unlettered,[73] and Priscilla says they are filled with childish fears."

Early the following morning, Mary lay curled up next to her mother for warmth. She longed for lolling[74] in a warm bed with no worries. Watching a slant of light filtering through the joints of the hatch door, she wondered what was going to happen to them. She was half awake when she heard Elder Brewster's voice.

"Goodwife Chilton, we are bringing your husband to be with you. He has been chilled with high fever all night and needs your help and comfort."

"Mary, arise and move over. We need to rearrange our sleeping area for your father," her mother said.

Though still half asleep, Mary moved to her hammock. She was groggy after a fitful sleep.

Elder Brewster assisted in laying Mary's father on the smoothed-out coverlet. "He has been shaking and cannot seem to get warm. Perhaps he will respond better here with you."

Mary knew her father had been ill and was relieved that he could now be with them. Goodwife Chilton felt his forehead, her love evident in her gentle touch.

"Mary, go fetch some of our water and rags."

"Mum, there is none to be found. What shall we do?"

Just then, Constance, who was awake from the commotion, came over and offered a piece of wet rag.

"Bless thee, dear child," Mary's mother said.

Goodwife Chilton placed the cool rag on her husband's pale forehead to wipe away the heat.

"Is Father going to be all right? Here, Mum, use my coverlet to add some comfort"

---

[73] **Unlettered:** illiterate
[74] **Lolling:** to waste time, aimless activity

"Mary, do not worry now. He is resting."

"Do not be fearful, Mary," Constance reassured her. "Your father is in everyone's prayers."

Just then, John Alden came down the steps looking for Priscilla. He squinted and walked forward at the same time as his eyes adjusted to the dark.

"Mary is that ye?" He cast her a brief look. "How is your father feeling?"

"Father is very hot and uncomfortable."

"I will try to find some water for him. Where is Priscilla?" He spotted her, and he smiled broadly as he greeted her. "There ye are!"

Mary was amused at how John forgot everyone around him but Priscilla. Mary listened unabashedly to John and Priscilla, who might have been completely alone for all the attention they paid her.

"I have carved something for Joseph." John placed a small boat in Priscilla's hands, and for an extra moment he held his warm hands around hers.

"Oh, thank ye. Joseph will so enjoy this!" Priscilla glanced down briefly and then quickly back into his eyes.

John and Priscilla's feelings for each other were no secret to the rest of the passengers. Mary and Constance often talked about the sweethearts, and watching their strange courtship was the best entertainment to be had in the middle of the ocean on a dark, damp, drafty ship.

"To have ye here below, within reach and yet out of reach—to meet ye this way, 'tis the very reverse of what I want," Priscilla said.

John looked briefly at the folks lying about, then paused again as he looked deep into her eyes, "I had better go now."

She lowered her head slightly with her eyes looking up at him.

"Dearest!" he said without moving.

Mary noted with great interest how Priscilla fluttered her eyes at John and stored it away for future reference. Perhaps the day would come when she would have need of such skills. Priscilla was much admired by everyone for the way she cared for her parents, and Mary quite looked up to her. In a way, she filled the empty spot that had grown in Mary's heart since she had waved good-bye to her sisters. Now Mary enjoyed watching Priscilla and John. They could have been the only two people on the ship for the scant attention they paid those around them. For a time, they continued to be absorbed in each other. Mary could see plainly in John's eyes the depth of his feelings for Priscilla, as well as Priscilla's own unspoken answer.

For a little while, romance had taken Mary's mind off their plight. Death was lurking in every corner of the bunks, and fear appeared in the fading eyes of the hungry.

"Hour by hour—that is how we are living," Master Mullins murmured out to his wife from the other end of the 'tween deck.

"Watch what ye speak!" snapped one of the irritated Strangers.

There was cause for serious concern, and patience was growing thin. As for the sick, some could not speak a word. For others, it was well-nigh impossible to remain silent.

One morning, Mary heard a muffled shout as she lay in her bed coverings. Looking over at Constance, she wondered if she was awake, and she strained to hear it again.

"Land ho!"

"Did I hear right?" Mary waved her arms to get Constance's attention and pointed upward, her eyes wide with excitement. "Let's go and see!" Mary whispered with a burst of energy.

Constance covered the baby, and the two girls rushed to the

ladder and tried to push the hatch open. Through the wood, they heard a muffled call.

"Land ho! Land ho!"

"At last!"

"Can it be?"

The announcement could hardly be believed! Shouts and whoops were heard on the deck above. The hollering was enough to wake the dead.

A sailor finally pried open the hatch wide and yelled, "Land has been sighted on the starboard side!"

Those who could tumbled from their sickbeds, covered with woolen coverlets, and cheered and wept. Some fell to their knees in prayer, rejoicing. Children began to jump and skip about.

It was November 11 on the sixty-seventh day since they left Plymouth, England. Mary's mother stayed with her father, who continued to lie very still. Mary and Constance wanted to pull off their soiled coifs and wave them high in the air in jubilation, but they knew better than to do such a thing.

Captain Jones cautiously threaded the *Mayflower* through the jutting shoals.[75] It was a challenging pattern of water the vessel encountered. Treacherous sandbars lurked below the surface in the curved harbor. Captain Jones maneuvered the large ship with confidence. He ordered the anchor be dropped into the hazardous waters and the sails lowered.

Mary could hardly believe her eyes. She and Constance wrapped and bundled themselves in their cloaks and hoods. Mary's smelled musty and stale, even in the cold, crisp air, but she had shrugged it off in resignation long ago. To bathe and douse herself in a tub of heated water had become one of her fondest wishes.

Mary breathlessly waved to Captain Jones, hoping for his

---

[75] **Shoals:** a sandbar forming a shallow place

approval to be topside. He didn't see her at first, but then he nodded and motioned Mary to come forward. Constance timidly followed behind. The captain led them to the forward deck.

Hopefully, Mary said, "Have we truly arrived, Captain Jones?"

"We are not certain. We need to explore the land, Mary." He appeared preoccupied with the sight of land. "Wait here and stay out of the way!"

The clouds were layered so no sun could break through to celebrate this day. The gray water was filled with swells as it lapped on the rim of the snow-lined shore. It was a morning of thick fog with the sound of far-off waves breaking into swells. Fog clung like tattered rags to the ironwood trees that spread along the spacious beach and farther inland.

Captain Jones now beckoned the girls to climb way up to the poop deck to have a better lookout. As they climbed, the wind was stronger. It seemed to Mary as she looked out that no civilization had ever touched this piece of land. The landscape looked like it would devour them. Thick forest spread as far as she could see in either direction, and everywhere except on the water, snow covered everything. The snow piled in drifts and blew like feathers when the wind was high.

Mary hurried back down to tell her parents the news. The heavy hatch door had absorbed so much moisture it was like opening a trap door. She stopped to get her bearings. Pulling her hood off her head, she peered in at the suffering 'tween deck, holding her nose to the stink as she adjusted to the dark and tripped over a random bundle.

A sudden flicker of light from a side passage guided her to her parents' tight corner where they had all been wedged together.

She took her mother's hand and breathlessly reported, "Master Brewster said we must not leave the ship. We only could watch from the deck. There is snow, and hundreds of trees—a real forest. And everywhere the cold, white snow is piled in mounds and drifts!"

"Shh," her mother sighed in a voice deliberately low.

But Mary's joy was contagious, and she gave her mother a hug. Her mother shared her happiness with a tired smile, yet her eyes showed concern and not a sound escaped her lips. Mary could tell she was worried about Father.

"Mary!" he snapped. She knew he was suffering by the impatient tone in his voice. Had he not been ill, he would have never raised his voice to her.

She turned with a slight glance of surprise at his tone.

"The water is seeping again. I should think a good size rag could be stuffed in that crack," he grumbled wearily.

"I'm so sorry, Father. I will plug it up immediately," she said, keeping her voice cheerful to comfort her father.

She reached up to push an old piece of linen in between the planks while her heart was pulled in two directions. Part of it was soaring over her new land, and part was weighted down like a ship at anchor at seeing how her parents were suffering. Still, they had arrived. Surely all would be well now.

Chapter 19
The Shadow of Death

HOW QUICKLY THEIR JUBILATION turned sour. Captain Jones was growing weary of the continual bickering among the sailors. The passengers and crew were experiencing outbursts and conflict among each other with each passing hour. To be in view of the New World but not able to leave the ship was a sore disappointment to all. The Pilgrim leaders decided before anyone could leave the ship that they would call an urgent meeting.

"Husband, tomorrow morning the leaders are calling a meeting to resolve these vexed feelings." Mary perked up her ears as her mother quietly told her father this.

Then what Mary heard next was something that she had always thought but never dared to express.

"Husband, dear, women have good insights and wisdom. Do you think our voices could be heard?"

"I know ye are wise, Goodwife, but women are excluded because they are not free agents. I doubt if things will ever change. Men are the ones to speak on important matters and decisions," her father replied with renewed strength.

Mary lay in her hammock thinking about what she had heard her father say—she felt that girls were just as clever as boys . . .

sometimes more clever, and certainly just as courageous. She wondered if things would be different someday in the New World.

By morning, her father began coughing and coughing—a spasm of fits it seemed would never stop. He could hardly catch his breath or even stand upright and needed assistance to gather with the other men in the captain's quarters. The women and children waited anxiously as they did their tasks: pitting the last of the prunes, mending the patches, and repatching everything yet again.

Mary's mother was grieving over the rivalry and dissension. "Heaven knows how few there are of us to colonize. Unity is vital. We must stay together in spirit and in loyalties."

She clasped her hands under her chin as if to whisper a prayer.

"Why are they taking so long, Mum?"

"We must try to keep our chin up and hope for the best. Besides dear, what good has worrying ever done?" Mary was aware her mother hadn't really answered her question.

Studying her mother, slumped over with hollow cheeks, she realized that Mother must have been giving her meager portion of food to sustain her father. When her father finally joined them, Elder Brewster and Master Mullins helped him back to his bed, so weak was he.

"I trust everything will be all right now," he told the women quietly.

"'Tis a good agreement. We call it the Mayflower Compact.[76] We stood with our fellow Pilgrims in a solemn gathering for the common good." Elder Brewster looked strained but relieved.

Mary pulled the covers over her father's chest, and he strained to speak. She rested against him and asked, "What is it, Father?"

---

[76] **The Mayflower Compact**: promised fair laws and gave the people the right to choose their own leader

"Elder Brewster is a comfort when fear grips the soul," he whispered.

She leaned over and kissed him on the forehead. "Close your eyes now and rest—I'm proud of ye, Father. 'Twas mighty of thee to go to the meeting."

Later, Captain Jones required all passengers who were able to come topside and hear the words of the compact and see the forty-one signatures of the Pilgrims, simple farmers, tailors, weavers, coppers, hatters, and others who had all come together in common cause.

THE MAYFLOWER COMPACT

In ye name of God, Amen. We whose names are underwritten, the loyal subjects of our dread sovereign Lord, King James . . . doe by these presents solemnly[77] and mutually in ye presence of God, and one of another, covenant[78] and combine ourselves together into a coeval body politick . . .

and by virtue hearof to enact,[79] constitute, and frame such just and equall lawes, ordinance,[80] acts, constitutions, and offices, from time to time, as shall be thought most meet and convenient for ye generall good of ye Colonie, unto which we promise all due submission and obedience.

---

[77] **Solemnly:** seriously

[78] **Covenant:** an agreement; to promise

[79] **Enact:** to pass a bill or law

[80] **Ordinance:** an order, a statute, or regulation

John Carver	Edward Tilley	Samuel Fuller
William Bradford	John Tilley	Christopher Martin
Edward Winslow	Francis Cooke	William Mullins
William Brewster	Thomas Tinker	Richard Warren
Isaac Allerton	John Rigsdale	John Howland
Myles Standish	Edward Fuller	Stephen Hopkins
John Alden	Thomas Rogers	Degory Priest
John Turner	Richard Clarke	Thomas Williams
Francis Eaton	William White	Gilbert Winslow
James Chilton	Richard Gardiner	Edmond Margesson
John Crackstone	John Allerton	Peter Browne
John Billington	Thomas English	Richard Britteridge
Moses Fletcher	Edward Doty	George Soule
John Goodman	Edward Leister	

November, in ye year of ye raigne of our soveraigne Lord, King James of England, France, and Ireland ye eighteenth, and of Scotland ye fiftie fourth, Anno Domini 1620.

Elder William Bradford, it was agreed, would be their governor and he read the document out loud. Each one had signed his name to set the rules in the agreement called the Mayflower Compact. Even the worst troublemakers signed the document, agreeing to create and abide by just laws that would be for the good of all.

"We are all in accord," Elder Bradford said.

Shivering in the cold, one by one, the men and women realized they had to stick together, or all might perish. Even the children understood that their hopes for a prosperous future lay in the compact. Mary represented her family as she looked upon the document. Captain Jones helped her find her father's signature.

"There, Mary. Do you see your father's name, *James Chilton?*"

As she looked at the parchment, a new sense of pride awakened in her, and a thrill raced through her, along with a feeling that this was a momentous day.

Eager to come ashore, sixteen men prepared the shallop to explore the land for a settlement and find some source of food. Later on board, the men recounted their adventure to the eager passengers. Captain Myles Standish had found a spring of water. He had called to the others, "Come and drink heartily—our first taste of water in this New World!"

Myles exclaimed to the eager listeners, "The water gave us as much delight as ever we drank in all our lives."

On Monday, November 13, the men worked in teams to clear the snow. The air was sharp as the big boys dug pits, and within hours, huge fires were built. Snow was melted in large kettles and a long-awaited wash day began. Women gratefully came ashore with their arms full of soiled linens, smelly clothes, and bedding to do the first much-needed washing of clothes. One kettle was reserved to steam fish, the other for laundry. The women shaved lye[81] soap into the water, then began scrubbing and beating and rinsing heaps of clothes until their hands were raw. It was hard, backbreaking work, and the clothes were little improved by being washed in such a

---

[81] **Lye**: any strong alkaline solution, used in cleaning

manner. "Twas a sheer waste of time, that's what it was!" came the exhausting reports and complaints back on the ship.

Word spread quickly that they would not be settling at this harbor. That left everyone feeling a little sober.

Firewood was gathered, and small amounts of scavenged berries and nuts were brought back to the ship. The men saw innumerable amounts of trees: oak, walnut, ash, holly, aspen, sassafras, cherry, plum, and some they had never seen before, as well as leeks and onions growing wild. They came upon what looked like an abandoned Indian village. The strange piles of sand in the village turned out to be an unexpected bounty—digging into the piles, they found baskets full of corn. With resources so scarce, the men were very glad to find this corn and brought it aboard the *Mayflower*.

Once, the men were set upon by Indians who carefully aimed and shot arrows at them from behind the tree trunks and bushes. The men, taken by surprise, fired back, and the Indians speedily disappeared. Fortunately, no one was hurt in the encounter, and the Pilgrims gave solemn thanks to God for being saved.

After days of exploring the surrounding area, they didn't see any Indians again, but Captain Standish and his men found too many inlets of seawater filtering into the clear streams. Soon, everyone realized that they would have to continue their journey to

find a safer harbor. But to most on board, any destination would be welcome after the voyage they had been through.

One night, Mary was drifting

off to sleep, thinking about Nana. Had she ever faced hardships like the Pilgrims? Since her dream, Mary had the uncanny feeling that her grandmother actually knew her and shared her same worries even though she had died many years before. Mary instinctively reached for her locket, only to find it wasn't around her neck.

Where could it have gone?

Then she remembered she'd put it in her deepest pocket with her treasures, wrapped in her little blue cotton handkerchief. She gave a sigh. When her father warned her about the sailors taking things, she had decided to hide it. She had pondered whether it was better to conceal her locket or cover it up. She finally decided the deepest pocket in her inner skirt would be the safest place.

It was during the calamity of the broken beam and the awful terror that spread through the ship that she could last recall feeling for her locket. Under the damp quilts, she fumbled through her skirts. Feeling for her pocket, she opened the flap and reached way down. Her little doll that Isabella gave her was safely there. Quickly, she stretched her thumb and fingers from corner to corner. She twisted and pinched the fabric, feeling her blue handkerchief, probing further. Yes, there was the silk cord . . . but no locket!

She couldn't believe it was gone!

"Maybe it's underneath me or when I finally stand up, it will tumble from my skirt!" Mary was sick with distress.

Then, all of a sudden, she discovered an obscure little hole! She shuddered at the thought. Recalling her steps, she had been everywhere, it seemed. 'Tween deck for sure and topside too. Her head started to swirl.

How could this have happened?

She quickly sat upright. It was pitch-black and impossible to see.

Perhaps it was in her bedding. She felt around her bedding with increasing panic.

The stirring awoke Mary's mother. "Mary, are ye all right?"

"Nay, Mum, I'm not," she said desperately.

"Are ye ill? What is it, me luv?" She reached for Mary.

"Mum, me locket." By now Mary was weeping. "I . . . I can't find it."

"Shh, Mary, we will find it in the morning."

"I will not sleep 'til I find it," she whispered tearfully.

Mary lay there suspended in her hammock as her mind walked quickly over the top deck, down the stairs, through the 'tween deck, and every nook and cranny of the ship. The night seemed endless. At last she could faintly see the pegs and planks through the early grayness of dawn. She had been wide awake all night long. Mary slid out of her hammock—not even her empty stomach and the chilly morning air could hold her back. Her thoughts were fixed on finding her locket. While everyone was still asleep, she quietly went to work.

"Where could it be?" she asked herself.

Lifting the corners of the heavy quilts and covers, spreading her hands inside and under everywhere—she was sure she would find it as her mind flashed back again.

She had hidden it safely away after the looks she'd received from the crew. She didn't own a fancy jewel box, only her secret pocket. Everyone else got clothes mended. Why hadn't she noticed the hole wearing through her own skirt pocket? By late morning, Mary tearfully called the little children around her and promised a reward to the child who could find her cherished pendant.

"We need to make ready and look everywhere."

With all those little eyes searching, how could they miss it?

"'Tis gold with delicate roses and an inscription on it," she described urgently. "I know one of ye will find it—just keep looking until ye do."

Hours passed, and no sign of her priceless locket. Mary dreaded telling her father. After all, he had passed it on to her, not offering it to her older sisters. Not only might he think she was frivolous and neglectful, but what if the shock of Nana's locket gone forever made him more ill than ever?

Soon Constance made her way over bedding and barrels to Mary. "Mary, Mary, I heard about your locket. What a wretched thing to happen!"

"Oh, Constance, I don't know what to do. I cannot breathe until I find it."

Constance gave her a hug. "I'll help you find it. It must be some-where."

Mary prayed in her heart that God would remember her and help her locate her locket. She knew that God helped those who helped themselves and that His grace would comfort her. "It has got to be somewhere." Mary was resolute.

With every step she took, she concentrated with her eyes flashing from left to right.

"It has got to be underfoot, toppled down or fallen into something; it's somewhere on this ship," she muttered to herself.

"We are still looking," little Joseph said.

Mary swallowed hard, "Ye are a dear boy. Thank ye."

"It could not just disappear," Mary's mother said as she rummaged around and shook out their bedding.

By now everyone was looking for Mary's golden locket. Anxiety and grief were getting the best of Mary, and her imagination was thinking the worst. "If it's found, surely no one would simply keep it, would they?"

"Mary, we must not think like that—who would want to do something like that, anyway?"

Mary looked and looked. If it had slipped from her pocket on the upper deck, it would have been washed out to sea by now. Mary wouldn't let herself think such a thought.

"Come, Mary, let's go topside. With luck we'll find it," Constance urged.

Mary took a deep breath and agreed. "All right."

The two of them pushed hard on the heavy hatch, opening it a little at a time. It looked clear enough, so the girls climbed up. High against the pale sky, seagulls soared and whined out as if they were mourning.

"With all the work the sailors have to do, who would even care? But oh, how I care!" Mary said, wiping away her tears. "With all the suffering on this ship, would anyone even begin to care about a lost locket?" Mary asked Constance in despair, sobbing as if her heart would break.

Constance put her arm around Mary's shoulders and pulled her close. "Don't lose hope, Mary."

Discouraged, Mary said, "It would be a miracle if it was found." Her eyes brimmed with new tears. "I was so foolish not to notice that my own pocket needed mending. How could I not notice that?"

"Mary, here, use my apron to wipe thy tears and nose."

It had been a long day. Just as the setting sun burned through the clouds, a young sailor scrubbing the deck worked his way over to the girls. He could have been only a year or two older than they.

"Me name is Hank," he said, his voice cracking.

The girls stepped back a few steps. No sailor boy had ever spoken directly to either of them. He seemed harmless despite looking rather disheveled. He gestured awkwardly with his hand. Mary blinked, and Constance pressed her teeth against her bottom lip.

"Me mate and I were scrubbing the deck," he stammered and reached into the fold of his knitted cap and held out his hand. "I found this fixed between the planks. Aye, 'tis a wee treasure for one of ye people."

Mary just stood there dumbfounded, unable to move. Her eyes already red from crying, blurred up again with tears.

Constance burst with excitement, "Mary, 'tis your locket!"

For a moment, Mary was speechless with joy.

Finally she exclaimed gratefully, "Thank ye, oh, thank ye!"

With a nervous grin out of the corner of his mouth, he placed it in her hand, and then went about his work.

While it had a small dent in it, right on the word "adversity," Mary didn't mind. The girls hugged each other tightly. Mary closed her eyes and whispered a silent prayer to God for a young sailor's goodness, and for Constance, whose concern and comfort sealed a lasting friendship.

"And to think we tried to torment those sailors. Oh, Constance, it makes me terribly ashamed."

Constance agreed. "We were judging the whole lot of them."

Wiping her eyes with both hands, Mary said, "Thanks be to God for one kind sailor boy." Mary sighed again. "Let's go tell me mum and all the children!"

After a few more weeks, they discovered the land curved around in the shape of a narrow neck.

"There will be no protection to our people," Elder Bradford wisely said. "We may not settle here near this beach and harbor at all, for it is ill-suited for shipping and unsafe for a settlement or colony."

Mary heard that the land actually was very narrow, with ocean on either side. There was more talk of sailing farther west. However, with the excitement of solid ground beneath their feet, they had already named it Provincetown Harbor. Their Sabbath days were spent in worship, and no one went ashore nor did work of any kind. Prayers continued to reach out for guidance. The hope and promise of a place to settle at last was fading away as was the sandy ground where they were anchored.

While confined on the *Mayflower*, Mary and her mother cared for her father. His fever made him alternate between delirium and a fitful, dreamless sleep. Master Chilton's worries, pleasures, and trials were already receding into the past. It had never occurred to Mary that she might lose him.

"Mum, it seems to me as if I should never have enough of looking at Father, or feeling the pressure of his hand upon mine," Mary said slowly. "Oh, Mum, do you think this misery will ever end?"

Her father seemed much older and very tired, almost defeated. Mary's bright spirit of adventure was slowly losing its glow. Would they ever come to the end of their journey?

Her mother's brow tightened as she said, "Everyone was wondrously happy and excited at the sight of land, but now the men are grim-faced, and everyone's world has shrunk to the size of their sleeping place."

She stroked Mary's head and said in a more comforting voice, "'Tis a fearsome time for everyone. In your adversities, ye will find God. That is how it has been for your father and me and your grandmother and many others. With God, everything is possible. Ye will find there can be much compensation[82] for suffering and hardships. We all move through trials, and they bring us closer to Christ. Let us kneel by your father and ask God for his guidance and mercy."

---

[82] **Compensation:** to make up for

On their knees, Mary and her mother could not seem to put their fears into words. Their hearts were earnest, yet their words seemed numb as they prayed for strength and comfort.

"Mary, dear," her mother said quietly, "we will do what we can do. After that 'tis done, we will figure out what to do next. No sense worrying. We will do our best, Mary, and angels above can do no better. For now, we are sorely needed here by thy father's side."

"Mum," Mary said quietly, "I will tend to Father's needs. Ye go up topside and breathe some fresh air."

Reluctantly, Goodwife Chilton wrapped herself up, telling Mary that she would not be long. Mary thought back on Leyden and the awful time her father had when he'd been attacked by hoodlums, and how her mother hastily sought relief for his pain and promptly assisted in his comfort. She had worried so, because he had been in excruciating pain and his head was throbbing and dizzy. It was as if she could recall every awful moment of that time. As terrible as that day had been, she had known that he would get well with her mother's care. Her thoughts continued on to Leyden, where she wondered about Remy and her friends; her big sisters, and her cat, Master Albert; the tidy, never-to-be-forgotten windmill castle . . . yet now, in the candle light, her father looked weary and hardly able to move.

Almost lifeless, he slowly reached for her hand. "Mary." He spoke softly.

"Father." Mary sank to her knees alongside him and kissed his hand. She looked into his half-closed eyes where shadows deepened the sockets. He seemed very fragile, and she could not bear to see him suffer.

"Mary, my child." His words were faintly slurred. "Ye must carry on in this new land." Hardly able to speak, he strained to continue, "Ye . . . have carried heavy burdens and . . . proved to be strong."

He paused, struggling for enough breath. After a long pause, his kind eyes moved slowly to Mary's locket, now back safely around her neck. He continued, "Sweet . . . are the uses of adversity . . . I . . . I love you, Mary, dear."

Mary's mother returned from the upper deck, rewrapping herself in an old coverlet to avert the draft, and sank down wearily on a nearby trunk.

Master Chilton reached for Mary. He seemed to see, even though his eyes were closed. He could see with his hands as he felt the beautiful features of his daughter's face, tracing her eyes and round, smooth cheeks. Then he rested his head back for a moment, and his breathing became shallow. Beneath his bare head, Mary could see the soft folds of a worn linen cloth Mum had spun in Leyden. It seemed the light of heaven approached as he uttered, "May God stay . . . between me and thee while we are . . . absent one from another." And with this, he took three long gentle breaths . . . and all was over.

Mary's mother gave a heartbroken wail, and the spirit went out of her as she slumped down.

Mary cried out, "No, Father, please no, do not leave us now!"

Mother and daughter clung to each other, sobbing. Mary wailed, "We are almost there in the New World, the world you dreamed and planned for us."

Her voice broke, "What will we do? We can't possibly manage without ye! Who will care for us? Oh, Mum!"

Mary's mother said between sobs in disbelief, "He looks so still."

Mary gazed at her father for a long time. He lay thin and pale with no more breath in his body. Fresh tears welled up in her eyes. In her mind she imagined heaven. *How does it all come together? His body is here*, she thought . . . *Could his spirit actually be in heaven?* Confused, she wept softly. How could all her family be lost forever? She had heard her father's last breath and waited and waited.

In disbelief, she groaned, "He will breathe, I know he will," and as if he could hear, she repeated helplessly, "Breathe, Father, oh, breathe!" Mary was inconsolable as she lay at her father's feet.

Elder Brewster came and gently lifted her limp body up into his arms, giving her comforting words. "Be still, Mary, God is near. He will never leave you comfortless."

The entire 'tween deck was silent. No one said a thing. They were so quiet—it was as if a little part of everyone had died. The only sound to be heard was Mary weeping for her dear father.

Chapter 15
Sweet Are the Uses of Adversity

NEITHER MARY NOR HER mother was prepared for the overwhelming task of burying a husband and father. Yet sadly, that was the next necessary thing to be done. His frail, slender body was wrapped in heavy canvas that was to be used for new sails, but out of respect for his elderly friend, Captain Jones had offered the weighty material. He wanted to help in any way he could, for he could see that young Mary and her mother were in deep anguish. Her father's body was carefully lifted to the top deck as Goodwife Chilton fell upon her husband's cold, empty bedding and wept and wept.

"I do not know how we shall fare without him." Tearstains outlined the dirt on her mother's pale cheeks as she uttered, "God help us!"

Plans were made to carry the body ashore for the burial. It was a solemn hour. Motionless, Mary and her mother stood dolefully, wrapped in heavy hooded coverlets, at the railing on the top deck. Ever since the attack by Indians, it was deemed unsafe for the women or children to go ashore. Instead, they watched the shallop make its way to the desolate, snow-banked shore. So thick were the pines that the morning sun barely touched the ground between them.

Emotion filled Goodwife Chilton's voice as she said, "Me heart is broken . . . yet, we shall never give up—that is how thy father would want us to carry on." Mary didn't know how she could do that, but she knew her mother was only trying to comfort her, so she squeezed her hand in support.

The whole procession trudged through the hard-crusted snow in somber silence. Brushing aside the drifts and hacking at the frozen topsoil with their cutlasses,[83] they dug deep enough to lay James Chilton to his final place of rest. The shrouded body, all carefully prepared, was lifted and carried, then lowered into the shallow grave, for that was the best that they could do in the bitter cold of winter. Elder Brewster offered a prayer of comfort. Heads were bowed as they huddled together amid the hollows of the dunes.[84]

Mary opened her tear-filled eyes for just a minute, straining to see. She wanted to capture the memory of her father's grave site. The cruel wind blurred her vision to where she could no longer see. A chill went through her body as she thought of her beloved father lying in that frozen corner of earth. She closed it out of her head, for it was a fearsome image to think of his once strong body under that cold, snow-covered ground.

In the days that followed, Constance and Johnny were the best kind of friends to Mary; comforting her and listening to her was healing at a time when Mary was numb and heartsick.

Constance waited for the right moment to say, "Mary, at birth, someone is there to receive ye. Then at death, someone is there to greet ye back home to God. 'Tis God's plan. Love for each other always lasts forever beyond the grave."

---

[83] **Cutlass:** a short, heavy, slightly curved sword with a single cutting edge, formerly used by sailors.
[84] **Dunes**: rounded hill or ridge

Johnny put his warm arm around her. "Me Mary," he said tenderly, "let thy tears be free in comin'. Grievin' is the price ye pay for love."

Mary, still downhearted, said, "Me father is in heaven with God, and Mum and I are left here. I feel so helpless and desolate. It seems indeed as if the Lord has forgotten us."

"Sometimes God brings us lower before He lifts us higher," Johnny said softly. He wiped her tears with his thumb.

Later, pressing her locket to her chest, Mary knew at that moment the most difficult burden lay yet ahead. Quietly, the two girls nestled around the warmth of the 'tween stove and tried to imagine what their homes would be like in such a dreary part of the world.

No one wanted to stay up on deck anymore to watch the men while they worked in the freezing cold. Everyone looked forward to Sundays when work was put aside and they could have a restful Sabbath of psalms and listen to sermons by William Bradford.

A barren wilderness offered no form of comfort to an already discouraged people. From a dark corner of the 'tween deck, a low voice mumbled, "We will be no better off out there than we are here on board."

Another spoke, "'Tis a vast, empty, silent land to greet us."

"Aye, except the savages. We saw five fine Indians coming toward us and they hid among the trees as soon as they sighted Captain Standish and our men."

This was an excitable subject, and everyone had a comment. The smaller boys sat with their eyes and ears wide open.

Another older boy promptly added, "The feathered men speedily disappeared when our men fired upon them. Our men then picked up the curious arrows. Some of them were arrowheads made with brass and others fashioned with eagle claws."

At that, Elder Brewster, a more visionary man, wisely calmed the group down. "As Pilgrims, we must continue to pray together that one day we will be able to make a fair and lasting treaty with the Indians when we are settled."

After many days and much thought, Captain Jones read maps and charts to find the ship's position. The ship had been blown off course. In the small room where the sea charts were kept and courses plotted, a meeting was called. Captain Jones showed a map from 1614, *A New World Coastline*, as he consulted with Elders Brewster and Bradford, John Carver, and his first mate.

"This area is called Cape Cod because of the fish hook shape," Captain Jones announced. "We are badly off course and too far northeast of our destination."

With confidence, he said, "We will cast off tomorrow and go forth to our new home."

Elder Bradford added, "Divine providence guided us to Cape Cod just in time to gather food for our starving people. We shall forever be grateful to God for the provisions gathered at Provincetown."

While at the Cape Cod Harbor and before they set out for their new destination, a disturbing tragedy happened. William Bradford had left on another three-day expedition. Everyone was so involved with illness and preparing the ship that no one saw Dorothy Bradford, his wife, slip under the open railing into the frigid water. Immediately she was missed, and no one could find a trace of the quiet young woman. Elder William Bradford and his wife, Dorothy, had made a difficult decision to leave their small son sobbing in the arms of his grandparents, in Leyden, until later when they were settled and they would send for him. Dorothy spent her time caring for many of the young children during the voyage, yet she longed for her own son, and soon the grief and loneliness showed in the way she moved and in the sad expression on her face. William's duties with the exploration party required him to be gone on several scouting trips. Often, she waited for him topside, but this day she would no longer be waiting. When it became apparent that his wife was nowhere to be found, William became increasingly frantic. "Please, somebody, tell me what has happened to her."

Mary felt a chill down her back, as she recalled seeing Dorothy climb slowly, dragging herself to the upper deck.

"I saw her," she called out desperately, sharing what she had seen.

"No, it can't be true," were the cries of anguish heard among the 'tween deck people.

Heads were bowed and knees were bent in sorrow. Surely no one would be so anguished that they would give up their own life; she most certainly had simply had an accident. Perhaps her foot slipped on the damp deck board, and she had hit her head slipping under the railing.

Captain Jones hurried William Bradford away from passengers to the master's cabin. After what seemed like a long time, William Bradford finally emerged. His footsteps were uneven and slow. He shook his head mournfully and seemed to stumble about, while wiping his eyes on his coat sleeve. They had come all this way together to start a new life. Mourning his beautiful helpmate, how would he face the future? He stayed in solitude in his cabin for several days. When he appeared, he seemed pale and somber . . . then he never spoke her name again. It was a spine-chilling tragedy, and yet it remained a strange mystery.

Mary and her mother felt Master Bradford's sorrow intensely and were shaken to the core all over again, as they felt the raw emotion of Mary's father's passing being relived. The two could hardly hold each other up nor keep from weeping.

"Poor man." Mary's mother knew only too well the loss. "No amount of sorrow can make things right. Only the Lord's love can do that if we will let Him."

The winter storms worsened. The ship pitched and fell into the depths of the sea, and with no medication and no fresh air to breathe, it was beyond what Mary could absorb. A suffocating fear welled up within her when she thought of all the hardships they had suffered, not to mention leaving the beautiful shores of Holland and England behind. Had it really only been a few months ago that they had been on the *Speedwell*, her father so excited to point out where they had once lived in the nearby village of Canterbury? Even though she couldn't remember it, she could picture in her mind the green fields and dells with meadows, with homes in Canterbury and Scrooby, where they had once lived peacefully with their family and friends . . . and then she thought of their beloved home they left in Leyden.

Mary had endured so many farewells, the creaking, overcrowded ship, the stormy seas, the death of her beloved father, and the ever-present hunger and thirst. She could not bear any more sickness or death. To have come so far, only to reach this cold, hard land, or even to perish within sight of it, seemed so hard. What did the future hold for them now? Would they live a brief life of hunger and pain, or would they survive and make a new home? Mary was tired deep down to her bones—tired of the endless cold and damp, tired of lack of sunshine and food and warmth, tired of fetching this and that. Even thinking of what must be done to build a new home in this strange, lonely land made her tired.

Her eyes were red and puffy as she pulled herself up the ladder and forced herself through the awful hatch that so often kept them imprisoned below and away from the fresh air on the main deck.

Constance wrapped up baby Oceanus and gave him to her mother and quickly followed after her. Mary was unable to endure it any longer. There seemed to be no end to this helpless feeling. She tried to find some small bit of hope in her heart, but she felt drained, empty. "Constance, what will be our fate? My courage is broken."

She pulled her hood tighter. Frigid wind whipped across the boat as the grief-stricken girls huddled together. With her chin quivering, Mary spoke softly, muttering, "Sweet are the uses of adversity . . . what more can we do?"

Constance was silent by her side, leaving Mary to ponder.

How did one use adversity? How could it possibly be sweet?

Straining to see through the gloomy, vaporous fog, Mary was lost in thought. In the cold, the girls comforted each other and pulled out a heavy canvas, which took the two of them to lift, and covered themselves from the endless exposure to the elements. They found a small cove-like corner inside the railing where they curled up, trying to keep warm.

With quiet concern, Constance said, "I'm sad, Mary. 'Tis not fair that your mum is sick now."

"Aye, my mum is terribly weak."

Constance leaned against her shoulder in loyal companionship. The sweet gesture sparked a little flame in Mary's heart. What a dear friend she had found in Constance.

Mary and Constance cared deeply about each other and valued their friendship more in this moment than they had ever thought possible. The glow in her heart burned brighter until Mary felt like she was sitting under a sunny sky. Looking up at the thick, gathering clouds and glancing around at the lifeless deck, it was as if she was seeing the world with new eyes.

Before she could take another breath, she heard herself whisper, "I know! I think I know now!"

For just a moment, she understood adversity better.

Mary didn't know how or why, but she tried to find the words to tell Constance. "'Tis much the same as when ye have been ill and then ye are well and strong again, on your feet even stronger than before." Perhaps she had learned to be patient . . . had learned to serve others and forgot herself through many hardships.

Then with no effort, the word *sweet* came to her mind, and this time it was more than a fleeting impression. She said out loud, "The world is a better place and even sweeter when we care for each other by reaching out during difficult times."

"Mary, methinks that is true," Constance said.

Mary paused for a thoughtful moment, and felt confidence bloom within herself. "I do feel better, Constance. I think I've realized what me little locket means! Like ye've said, we must never doubt nor fear; otherwise, we let sorrow rob us of faith."

Together, they knew that everything was going to be all right. A soft light fell from above and sprinkled the heavenly sky with stars. The full moon shifting through the clouds gave a gentle glow on the heads of two unspoiled, untouched little Pilgrim girls.

Later that evening, Mary had just dozed off to sleep when she was startled awake. In the dark, she held her breath, straining to hear what had woken her. There it was. Muffled footsteps, a stifled laugh, and then someone making a hushing sound. Only one small lantern in a corner cast any light in the gloomy shadows of the 'tween deck. The hairs on Mary's neck prickled. A still, small voice warned her to hold still. She opened her eyes a crack, and almost gasped out loud at what she saw. Francis and John Billington, sneaking past her hammock, and in John's hands, the barrel of a musket gleaming dully in the faint light.

Mary didn't move until the brothers had moved past her. Her heart raced. What were they up to? It couldn't be anything good. She had to let someone know, but who? Everyone on the women's side was fast asleep. Perhaps she should make her way over to the men's side and try to find Elder Brewster in the dark. If only she could rely on her father, but there was no point in wishing for the impossible. She had to act now! The warm feeling that had woken her and warned her now urged her to get up, hurry to the hatch, and push it open. Usually, she had to have Constance's or Johnny's help to push the heavy wood covering up, but now she opened it effortlessly.

In her mind, she knew exactly what she needed to do. Hurry to the captain's quarters. Normally, she would have been too shy to even think of this, but tonight she was filled with a fiery confidence, as if a flame was burning in her heart. Upon first spotting the boys, she had been momentarily scared, but now, she was fearless. She ran straight to the great cabin where the captain slept, ignoring one old seaman who shouted, "Hey now, what're ye up to, missy?" and pounded loudly on the heavy oak door. It opened so abruptly that Mary stumbled right into Captain Jones.

"What in tarnation?" he said. "Mary, my child, what is the matter?"

"Oh, Captain Jones, begging thy pardon, but I fear something terrible is about to happen." With that, Mary quickly explained what she had seen, the boys sneaking off in the direction of the magazine—the section of the ship that housed the six great iron cannon for protecting the *Mayflower*. Besides the cannon, there were several caskets of gunpowder.

The captain didn't hesitate for a second. He took off at a run, hollering to the seamen on duty, with Mary right on his heels, down the hatch, through the aisle that separated the men's and women's quarters, to the stairs that led to the lower level. By now, all the commotion had people stirring in their hammocks and sleeping areas.

Just then, they felt a startling sensation that gave a shattering blast and jolted the entire ship! The smell of gun smoke seeped into the passageway and swirled around the deck. Everyone was suddenly terrified and screaming. People ran aimlessly, falling over and dodging round things as total panic broke out. In a flash, Jones raced down the stairs. He was raging as he searched for the location of the blast.

All thoughts of proper behavior for a young lady had left Mary's head. The only thing she could think of was helping to save the ship and her fellow passengers. In the smoky magazine room, a small blaze was burning. Captain Jones pulled off his heavy officer's coat and began to beat at the flames. Mary whipped off her apron and joined the captain. Several seamen joined the efforts and in short order, the flames were out before they could reach the gunpowder caskets.

To think the ship was almost destroyed by the two Billington boys!

"Wherever ye are, we'll catch ye!"

A gruff seaman bellowed out, "Which way did they go? Listen fer 'em!"

Fury shot from the captain's eyes. The shameful duo scampered through a narrow passageway at right angles that led them into another corridor. Deep in the bottom of the ship, the search was on.

"We'll track ye down!" The first mate promised in a nasty tone. His cold eyes were reduced to slits.

The captain waved his arm to the crewmen to follow him. "You'll never hide from us, ye scoundrels!"

The notorious boys scuttled along the wooden wall of the ship and disappeared.

Looking at the passengers now gathered around, the captain cried, "Which way did they go?!"

The two undoubtedly thought they were safe when at last they took refuge in two deep, empty barrels. But their panting gave them away; the echo inside those old wooden wine barrels disclosed their hiding place.

"Listen for 'em!" A crewman hollered.

"What's that?" said the first mate, cupping a hand to his ear and feeling in the dark with his other.

"Ahh, I found 'em!"

"Ye there!" shouted the captain. "Stand fast!"

There was no escaping as their wicked faces popped out. They froze on the spot with their eyes a big as beef pies.

"Do ye not have a sense between ye?"

The two were dim-witted enough to jump out and try to make a run for it.

One of the husky crewmen snatched them by the backs of their necks, "Do ye want to see the guillotine,[85] do ye?"

"Keep a wrathful hold on 'em," snarled another.

"Better do what the captain says, or he'll string ye up by your bloody ears!" warned the first mate.

Captain Jones stomped back up spitting with rage. The two rotten boys were dragged up to the main deck.

One woman called out, "Pity about you!"

Another cried, "Poke his eye!"

---

[85] **Guillotine:** an instrument for beheading

And yet another, "I do not think they will see through the night!"

With an angry oath, Captain Jones cuffed both boys soundly and dragged the scoundrels by their ears.

"Ye set my teeth on edge!" He spared nothing as he lectured them.

Goodwife Chilton complained, "Those dreadful, willful young'uns." She spotted Mary standing a little dazed now that the danger was past and went pale at the sight of her daughter smudged in soot and holding the burnt remains of her apron. "Dear Lord above. Mary, art thou injured?"

Mary shook her head, and the captain, still holding each of the Billington boys by an ear, said loud enough for all to hear, "'Twas the lass that warned me o' the mischief these hooligans were about. If not for her, surely we'd be in fearsome danger now."

Mary blushed at the captain's words of praise and was soon the center of attention while the captain hauled the Billington boys away for punishment.

Goodwife Chilton pulled Mary close and embraced her. "My dear girl, no mother could ask for a more honorable daughter."

Everyone wanted to hear the story, so Mary started at the beginning and told it all. Then Constance showed up after shushing Oceanus back to sleep from all the ruckus, and Mary had to tell the story again.

Goodwife Hopkins spoke out, "Praise the Lord that sent his angels to awaken ye, Mary. Those horrible boys have given us such a start. It will be good riddance to those little hoodlums!"

"They jeer their elders while tossing scraps and bones wherever they please!" Mistress Mullins added, "Glory be, and steal rations from the wee ones!"

Another said, "Aye, those good-for-noth'n boys, they need a sound beatin'!"

Word passed through the 'tween deck as more of the Billingtons' mischief came to light. "With their fists full of duck feathers, they filled the quills with gunpowder and made firecrackers!"

"Aye," someone else joined in, "most of the gunpowder was spilled on the floor, and the slightest spark could have set us on fire and exploded the entire ship!"

Another passenger added, "Those fools took the old musket hangin' on the wall and with one shot they nearly blew up the whole ship, almost injuring or killing us all!"

Elder Bradford said, "'Twas by the mercy of God that they just missed the deadly gunpowder keg."

"I've never known such a run of bad luck," Master Hopkins exclaimed, shaking his head, as he came to comfort his family.

Mistress Hopkins promptly said, "They have now been thrashed within an inch of their lives, those boys, this time by their own father. I doubt they shall ever do a bad deed again!"

It was only a few days later when Constance found Mary in a state of anguish. "Mary, we've heard your mother was taken to her bed," she said with concern.

"Mum is fearfully white and in a state of fatigue. Her strength has ebbed away," Mary said, her worry evident in her voice. "Elder Brewster said a prayer for her today and brought her some hot drink."

Goodwife Hopkins came near, putting her arm around Mary, "He always helps us in our time of trouble. He is watchful for the comfort of others," she said reassuringly.

"Aye, he looks past his own trouble and pains, so that those around him may be soothed, God bless him," Mistress Mullins added in a comforting tone.

"Captain Jones says to brace ourselves, a storm is coming," Master Mullins grimly announced.

Mary took a good look over the entire 'tween deck, took a deep breath, and wondered if they could survive another storm.

Constance rubbed her belly and said, "I'm so weary of hunger pangs that the very sight of these revolting morsels given to us sickens me more."

"Aye, Constance, I know—me as well."

Little Joseph, once an energetic lad, now lay pale, down with quinsy.[86] The Mullins family was in constant prayer for his well-being.

"Poor children!" Goodwife Hopkins said in despair. "With so much sickness, Christmas will not be a very cheery one, I fear."

Until she mentioned it, the children had not given it a thought.

"Sinterklaas comes to Holland," Mary said with a knowing smile, sitting with her legs curled beneath her and happy to pass along new information to the English passengers who didn't know anything about customs in Holland.

She had known of this tradition every year and for a long time wondered why Sinterklaas never came to their house. Then Mum explained one day that Christmas was a sacred day for them—not a day of festivities.

Mary continued, "And, if the Dutch children have been good, he leaves a delicious, juicy orange in their klompen—that's their wooden shoes!"

With those thoughts lingering in her mind, Mary thought about her sisters and how she missed them and prayed that Master Albert was safe and happy, catching mice in her sister's home.

"I shall miss the red holly berries and hymns of the Savior that we sang in England," Mistress Mullins spoke up.

---

[86] **Quinsy**: early term for tonsillitis

"Evergreens in the homes in winter represent a gift of everlasting life," Mistress Hopkins chimed in. "I fancy this Christmas to be our most blessed one. I am sure we will find evergreens in abundance. What more could we wish for than a home of bliss in the New World!"

With that thought everyone quietly agreed.

Their happy expressions soon vanished under the onslaught of another gale. The wind began to whistle and swirl with an unnerving noise. Mary climbed up into her hammock, waiting for the storm to hit. Peering over the rim, she could see down the length of the 'tween deck, over the heads of passengers bracing themselves for the storm. She looked at the Hopkins family to her left and the Mullins gathered together along with others sitting in ill-fitting clothing, holding well-worn coverlets folded in their arms and around their shoulders, their faces drawn and tired but with their Bibles opened and singing softly an old hymn.

> Now thank we all our God with hearts and hands and voices,
> Who wondrous things hath done, In whom his earth rejoices;
> Who from our mother's arms, Hath blessed us on our way
> With countless gifts of love, And still is ours today.
> Oh, may our bounteous God, Through all our life be near us,
> With ever joyful hearts, And blessed peace to cheer us,
> And keep us in his love, And guide us day and night,
> And free us from all ills, Protect us by his might.

Mary could see tears welling up in eyes as she listened intently to the words for the first time and thought how humble, how amazingly trusting these voices were, being raised to God in grateful prayer. They had scarcely anything, lacked in everything, yet not one wanted to murmur against God.

"Sweet are the uses of adversity" she said softly to herself. *Having faith in God makes us stronger and more worthy of His grace.* She realized how fragile liberty was that people were willing to give their very lives for freedom to think, worship, and believe as they wished. No wonder her father knew that there was more in this life for them. He had an eternal perspective of who they were as a family and what possibilities lay ahead for his posterity. She thought, *We are not just building a new colony . . . the Lord is building us!*

Waves soon began to gather, mounting in force, crashing into the tiny *Mayflower* with its sails snapping and weathered timber cracking. Every bit of wood was straining and creaking. By now everyone knew how to hold on with all their might. The tempest caused water to pour through the already leaking hull. The cold, wet, sick, dispirited Pilgrims nestled together, holding on in the pitch-black darkness. Mary made sure their little window was closed tight. She couldn't find a way to rest, and from the sounds around her, she could tell everyone was terrified by the prospect of yet another violent storm. There were fresh waves of sorrow and sobs again, for no one ever got used to such hurly[87] and discomfort. It was the kind of fear that none of them would ever forget.

Mary heard Master Mullins shouting to his wife, "I heard a sailor topside say, 'Hope yer prayers will keep us safe.' They are becoming a humble lot."

The weary Pilgrims offered up prayers mightily for the captain and his crew for yet another miracle to allow their only security, the *Mayflower*, to be guided through another tempest. Still, there were some quiet, hopeless sobs of fear. Mary thought about Johnny and the storm that they rode out together and hoped that he was all right; she had not seen him since the blast on the ship.

---

[87] **Hurly:** commotion

Mary slipped from her hammock to join her mother, and she snuggled and slept beside her for meager warmth and comfort. Her soft sleeping sounds gave Mary some reassurance, but tonight she was tortured by hunger, and she was frightened by the wind that roared through the rigging and angry waves that swept across the deck. She heard every sound, including the one or two who cried out sharply in their sleep.

Early the next morning, Mary instantly opened her eyes. The ship was absolutely still, and there were no sounds from the floor above. The storm had passed. Her mother had slept through the night in spite of the pounding storm. In an instant, Mary heard abrupt noises above on the top deck. She had learned to identify them, but this time the brisk sweeping movement seemed different. She tuned her ear, then without warning came a loud, exuberant shout.

"Land! Land ho!"

Chapter 16
"Mary, Mary of the Mayflower"

SHIPMATES CLIMBED THE RIGGING as ropes snapped. The whole ship came alive, and those who were able climbed to the main deck. Mary finally collected herself and jumped to her feet, grabbing a coverlet and climbing as fast as she could go. Her heart swelled with new hope when she saw the pale thin line of land. Around her, many faces were again wet with tears. This time the land looked solid and fast, unlike the sandy spit of land at Provincetown. Simple and gentlefolk the Pilgrims were, but their will and courage were no less than that of the most brave and weathered sailor.

Excitedly, Mary hurried down below deck to tell her mother. She leaned over to kiss her mother's troubled forehead, and she was bursting with excitement.

"Mum, Mum, 'tis true, we can see the New World again! I'm anxious to go ashore. 'Tis exciting to think that this is where we shall live, and I will marry and have my children!" Mary could hardly contain herself.

The sails smacked into position, and the anchor went down with a rattle of chains that drowned out nearly everything as they splashed into the dark, unexplored sea. The crew immediately lowered the shallop. Ready to explore, the landing party wasted no time in climbing aboard. The *Mayflower* lay in the open sea as weary Pilgrims crowded the railing, and children squeezed in between to see for themselves. There was not a soul in the bleak wilderness to welcome them; only a relentless and rock-bound coast awaited their small, disarming boat. The whine of winging seagulls gave a lonely offshore greeting. A ragged string of wild geese passed overhead, high in the gray sky. Most everyone was sick and coughing; wrapped in heavy woolen coverings or coats, mufflers, and hoods, they watched as the shallop landed and their courageous menfolk crawled out of the boat and knelt in prayer on the sandy shore to give thanks.

"O God, our Heavenly Father, we bless thy name for having brought us over this vast and furious ocean safely to the New World," was their fervent prayer of gratitude. Elder Bradford simultaneously gathered the Pilgrims below in the 'tween deck for a prayer of thanksgiving.

He told them, "Our children and grandchildren someday will rightly say our fathers were Englishmen who came over this great ocean, and were ready to perish in this wilderness, but they cried unto the Lord because He is good and His mercies endure forever."

Mary made her way back onto the deck, savoring the pine-scented breeze that lingered after the storm. She breathed in the land smells of the earth and trees mixed with the sharp, salty aroma of the sea and sandy coast. The many soaring birds crying and wheeling above their heads added to the merry excitement. Mary looked down into the water that lay between the ship and the sandy beach and then toward the forest, which was shimmering with wet mist. A gentle breeze blew strands of hair away from her face, and she tucked them back into her coif as best as she could. Mary squinted her eyes to see the treetops. Her eyes rested on a large rock that broke through the smooth, sweeping beach. Behind this rock rose a prominent hill, so she could not tell what lay beyond that. On one side, she saw a stream flowing through a deep gully and a great marsh that extended south to the river, then a hill on the other side, then the harbor, and again her eyes swept back to the large rock. While she knew that they might encounter Indians, she did not see movement of a living thing.

During the next few weeks the men explored the coastline and surroundings for exactly the right place that would meet all their needs. They sharpened their eyes to catch any sign or sound of the feathered men they knew were hidden in the depths of the forest. Shelter would be the next concern. All the young men would be needed for that, as most of the leaders had weakened alarmingly during the past weeks, some too weak to wield ax or adz[88] in their present condition. If there were natives present, would they be friendly and allow them to settle peacefully . . . or would they attack and even capture them?

They felt the will of God had proven providential in leading them to this particular landing site. A better place could not have been chosen. Men brought back armfuls of pine boughs, sweet-smelling herbs, and other treasures from the New World soil. This only made Mary long to go ashore and feel a freedom she had never known.

She put her hands to her face and closed her eyes and, giving a deep sigh of relief, said to herself, "Look out there, the New World. How it fills my heart. My whole life is waiting on that shore for me!"

Johnny was close by taking care of duties on the ship. When he spotted Mary he cried out, "Hooray!" in a jubilant voice.

"This is the best time of me life! I dreamt about America, and there it is right in front of me eyes—I can feel it, I can breathe it!"

---

[88] **Adz:** an ax like tool for dressing wood

Mary laughed at his enthusiasm, and he continued with a teasing smile, "Is me face as dirty as yers?"

"Aye, it is, Johnny." Her eyes sparkled, and her cheeks were as rosy from the sea-breeze as from the feelings that Johnny's presence stirred.

With a big grin from ear to ear, he went on saying, "Look at me, all salt-stained from top to bottom!"

"Ah, Johnny, you're a sterling fine lad, ye are! Ye'll make your own way all right. Ye'll do well here."

With a shrug he promptly responded, "As will ye. I wish I were like ye."

"Like me?" Amused, she rolled her eyes and turned her head.

"Aye, Mary, ye're not afraid of anything."

Completely catching her off guard, he took her hand and kissed it. "Ye quite amaze me."

The warmth of her smile held Johnny's eyes. Maybe it was because they were chilled or just excited, but at that instant they gave each other a robust hug. At that moment the world stood still and Mary felt a tenderness she couldn't put into words welling up inside her. Judging from the look in his eyes, she guessed Johnny was feeling the same. Johnny took her by the hand and tugged her to the rail, where they stood in silence for a long time, watching the shores of their new home and longing for the day they could set foot there.

Winter, it seemed, would not lose its hold. As yet, none of the women or children had been ashore. Men departed on the shallop early each morning, except Sunday. They worked as fast as they could to gather driftwood and chop trees to build fires and to build a common house. For most of the winter, with Captain Jones's goodwill, the women and children continued to live on the anchored ship. Mary chafed at the restriction and could hardly wait to feel the soil under her feet. Captain Jones agreed to the use of the *Mayflower* as a protected place until shelters were built. He would wait until spring to return the *Mayflower* to England.

One evening, tiny Oceanus' pitiful cry could be heard throughout the length and breadth of the 'tween quarters. Even as Constance tried to comfort him, he remained fretful, whimpering often and needing frequent attention. She came over next to Mary, with him in her arms and sat rocking him back and forth in the hammock.

"He's so hungry, poor little mite," Mary reached out. "Here, let me care for the babe. I'll hold him for a while." While she tried to give him relief by letting him suck on the tip of her finger, John Alden came down the hatch steps and walked boldly over to Priscilla. Mary watched with interest. He held out his hands full of pine needles and glossy green leaves adorned with red berries. "A gift." In the dim light Priscilla rose quietly to meet him, her outstretched hands acting as a guide to him.

"Priscilla, I have brought you something from the New World. It takes the place of a bouquet, perhaps it's like the English hawthorn flowers that bear a promise."

There was no need for words between them. The love in their eyes spoke volumes. Mary had a feeling the *Mayflower* would return to England without a certain cooper on board. Priscilla set the berries and fragrant pine needles aside and burst forward with a bright smile, and John wrapped his arms about her and pressed his lips gently to hers. Oceanus sighed, and so did Mary as she dreamed about the day when a certain young man might court her.

Death was becoming more and more a part of their lives.

"What a difference it would have made in all of our dreams if we could have arrived even a month or two earlier," Mary's mother said. Now the days and nights were short, cold, and bitter. The fire would not burn or even catch hold of the wood that was so green and wet.

"Shh, Mum, everything is going to be all right. Remember in the Bible where it tells us, 'Trust in the Lord with all thine heart. In all thy ways acknowledge Him, and He shall direct thy paths?' I feel as if we have been restored to the favor of God. I pray that He will forgive my murmuring and will give me patience to endure waiting on this ship!"

Out of nowhere, Mary could feel a draft of severe, brutal cold from above that set her teeth chattering. Constance and some of her friends eagerly called her from topside. They had pulled opened the hatch and were peering down through the opening and were excitedly calling her to come quickly.

"Mary, Mary, Captain Jones is beckoning ye!"

Hastily, she pulled a woolen shawl about her shoulders and climbed through the hatch as her friends held the heavy door open.

As Mary stood before Captain Jones she gave a bit of a curtsey out of respect and wondered if she had done something wrong. "Sir? Sir, I apologize if I, I . . ."

Mary felt her heart pounding out of her chest, not sure what to expect. In the presence of Captain Jones, the children always felt that he knew everything they were up to and that perhaps even the shipmates kept him informed. Constance stood behind Mary and gave her a poke in the back with her finger. It was no secret that the children had been rambunctious and into mischief since arriving in Plymouth Harbor. By now, Captain Jones and Mary had locked eyes. Everything she and Constance had ever done aboard the *Mayflower* went racing through her head.

Still, she knew that Captain Jones had felt fatherly toward her at times, especially since her father died.

But there was no denying he was a stern man. Had that special bond she felt with him suddenly disappeared? She knew that he was fond of her, wasn't he? So what was this all about?

"Don't rush to apologize, lass. Ye've done nothin' wrong," he said with his usual cutting voice.

With her eyes wide open, Mary held her breath, biting her lower lip. Captain Jones stood there and stared down at her. Mary swallowed, blinked her eyes, and nodded all at the same time.

"Mary," he paused, "to honor your good father, James Chilton, and his fine name, and his family, and in recognition of your quick thinking when we were in danger, I wish to announce that ye may have the good pleasure, early tomorrow morning, to attend the next departing shallop!"

Mary was stunned but immediately cried out with delight. Jumping up and down, she couldn't keep her excitement inside. Her eyes flashed with wonderment and filled with tears. For such a proposal to be made was highly unheard of. The cold wind blew her tears and locks of hair around her face. After a moment, she was aware that everyone was looking at her and she realized that she was in for a great adventure and so soon . . . in the morning! For such an unusual summons from the captain, her heart swelled with gratitude and pride as she thought of her father and mother. She could also feel the unseen heart and hands of her beloved Nana reaching out to her. But, best of all, now she could climb out of this smelly ship!

"Constance, I will come back and tell ye everything."

"I will hold good thoughts for ye, Mary. Remember when we told each other one day we would have our homes and children here?" She stretched out her arms as if to welcome and embrace their future!

"I do remember, Constance. It's all coming true! Look afar out there. Notice the small creek running along? That's where I wish to have my cottage—do ye see where I am pointing?"

"Aye, Mary, look to the right; there is space for two cottages and one big herb garden to share. I can almost see it as if it's already there with vines of berries, hollyhocks, and foxglove!"

Mary smiled and said, "We are full of notions and castles in the air and yet such girls."

"We will need protection and God to provide us with good husbands," Constance noted.

"Aye." Mary smiled. "But before that, we will need God's grace to help us to help ourselves."

The two girls hugged tightly and knew they had a loyal bond that would last no matter what would happen.

Early the next morning a layer of misty fog lay waiting on the surface of the ocean as a thin light burst through, showing the tranquil sea that turned from gray to a mild blue with the sun's pale rays spread out over the water. The shallop was ready to be launched. Mary had hardly slept. She was wide awake the entire night thinking about stepping foot onto the new land.

"With God all things are possible." It's not sweet like honey, she told herself. *Adversity is sweet . . . because it makes you strong and courageous, that's why it's sweet.*

Thinking about her father's vision for freedom gave her strength and courage and renewed pride in him. He would want her to carry on. The very thought of being the first girl to go ashore was beyond her imagination.

"Mum, are ye sure ye'll be all right if I go? I will come back soon and be with ye," she promised.

With caution in her voice, her mother said, "Mary, dear, keep as warm and bundled up as ye can, preserve better walking, and hold on tight, the sea is rough. Go with me blessing and enjoy this to thy soul's content. Do be careful, Mary."

They held each other for a moment before she kissed her mother good-bye. Mary knew that she must press forward and be steadfast with a perfect brightness of hope and love of God. She recalled something her father said: "For each generation needs to be stronger than the last." She knew the sweetness she felt was renewed strength that would help her to endure whatever the future would bring.

Wisps of fog hung in the air while Mary descended down into the shallop. Under the captain's watchful eye and command, the shallop pushed off into the iron-cold water. The sky was an unusual pink at the horizon that blended into gray. Huddling together at the railing, shipmates and friends watched from the *Mayflower* and gave jubilant calls that carried out over the open sea. The *Mayflower* was anchored about one-and-half miles out in the bay. While men maneuvered the paddles, Mary sat toward the front of the boat. She spied that big rock again. Mary had become fortified and unmovable like that rock. All that she and others had endured during their harrowing voyage rushed through her mind. Glancing back at the ship, she could see her friends waving and shouting cheers, and a familiar voice shouted out.

"Mary, Mary of the *Mayflower!*"

It was Johnny. With a joyful smile, she threw him a kiss and took a deep breath. It was bitterly cold as the stiff wind whipped across the open boat, cutting like a knife as the shore drew near. The tide had flooded in so they could not land on the beach. Sea spray froze on her heavy clothes like steel. Her fingers were frozen stiff, and her legs were wobbly after so many weeks at sea.

Approaching the water's edge, the rock became immense in size and perfect for stepping ashore. Mary held her head high. With a smile on her lips and the freezing air flying in her face, she said to herself, "I will be first to step on that rock!"

Even though her legs felt numb, she felt a surge under her feet as the shallop pulled closer to the massive rock. A sudden impulse came upon her as the boat thudded into the sandy bottom of the shore. All the long months of waiting, all her hopes and fears and dreams overflowed, and she could no more stay in the boat than a wave can stay on the sand.

Mary gathered her skirts and leapt into the shallow water with a splash, wetting her feet. She waded knee-deep, reaching out to grasp hold, and then climbed up onto that giant boulder!

Though unaware of it at that moment, young Mary Chilton became celebrated, for she was the first woman to set foot onto Plymouth Rock,[89] in the land of America, a land filled with promise. Mary stood there on top of that great boulder and waved her shawl wildly in the air to signal to her friends that she finally had both feet on the land of liberty and freedom!

Weeks later, after Mary's dramatic leap, more tired wanderers made their way to the seashore as the waves lapped and pushed them onto the sandy shore. The shallop brought boatloads over the crashing waves. Grateful prayers were uttered right there on the wet sand. They knew that they were free to live their lives far away from oppression and despair forevermore.

---

[89] **Plymouth Rock**: the big rock that came to be known as Plymouth Rock was hallowed after the Pilgrims arrived. Even today it is a symbol of their landing.

Epilogue—November 1621

NOVEMBER IN NEW ENGLAND could be cold and gray, but today the sun was bright, turning the remaining leaves ablaze. The sun warmed Mary's back and reached all the way to her heart. For the first time in a long time, she felt happiness stirring in her soul.

The previous winter had been so hard and bleak. Barely half the Pilgrims had survived. The bitterest moment had come when her mother had held her hand and said, "Promise me ye'll not grieve long, my child. Remember: Weeping may endure for a night, but joy cometh in the morning." She gave Mary a little smile and closed her eyes for the last time.

Mary's long night had lasted all winter, as the cold, the lack of food and shelter, and illness had claimed one life after another. Little Eleanor More had died a few weeks after Goodwife Chilton, followed all too soon by her sister Mary and brother Jasper. Each was a blow to Mary's heart. Through it all, Constance and Johnny were ever by her side, sharing in her grief and comforting her in those dark days. One day Johnny left them too, succumbing to a sudden fever.

Would the morning never come? Where was the sweetness her locket promised? For a while, Mary thought that she would never be happy again. Still, Father would have been proud. Like a reed in the storm, Mary bent, but did not break. In her darkest hours, Mary found comfort. She felt her parents watching over her from somewhere just out of reach. She found new strength and courage. She became more aware of the beauty of nature and the treasure of friendship and family. Constance became like a sister, Richard like a younger brother. She would never stop missing her parents, and she would pray that someday she would see her sisters again, and perhaps even Master Albert. But until then, she was bonded with those who had survived the terrible first winter, a bond that would last as long as she lived.

"Mary, Mary!"

Richard came running into the vegetable garden where Mary was picking carrots and turnips for the evening stew. Richard barely paused to pant out his message and was off again in a flash. A ship had been spotted in the harbor! Mary dropped the carrots in the dirt and followed Richard, running all the way to the beach. It had been over six months since the *Mayflower* had departed, and many in Plymouth had wondered how long they were to scratch a colony out of the wilderness on their own without new supplies and helping hands.

Breathless, Mary stared at the ship, anchored now in the bay. A shallop was just being lowered, and by the time it landed on the beach, nearly every one of the fifty-three remaining colonists had already gathered by the water's edge to greet the newcomers.

There was such a fuss of cheers and greetings and hugs and handshakes. Some of the new passengers were family members of the *Mayflower* group, so there were more than a few tears as well. Mary noticed a striking young man with a cheerful grin and dimples that pinged her heart and reminded her of Johnny, for some reason, even though he looked nothing like him. Everyone shook everyone's hands, friend, family, or stranger alike, for in this harsh New World, so far across the sea from the rest of the world, they were all family in a way. So soon Mary was passed from greeting to greeting and found herself smiling into the face of the young man.

"Greetings, lass. I'm John Winslow, and pleased I am to be met by such a pretty face. If I had known the New World would have such beauty in it, I would have come over on the *Mayflower*. But my brother Edward had all the good fortune to go in my place. Mary blushed to the roots of her hair and laughed at his charming nonsense. She curtsied and told him her name, and they were both off to the next greeting. But his smile and his cheerful banter warmed a part of her heart that had fallen so cold when Johnny died.

There was much yet to be done, and surely hard days and years were still ahead. But there was also hope and the possibility of new friends and new joys. They would never replace the memory of those lost, but they would add their own fullness to life. Mary remembered the night she had witnessed John and Priscilla's love and dreamed of a love of her own one day, a family of her own, a home and freedom and hope . . . and had the first real glimmer of what her locket promised. No matter what lay ahead, life was going to be wonderful.

Laughing and talking with Constance by her side, Richard chattering happily away on her left, and a handsome young stranger with dimples looking back over his shoulder at her once or twice, she made her way back up the hill to her home and her future.

What Became of Them?

ALTHOUGH RECORDS FROM the early years of America are rare, we do know a few things:

Mary married John Winslow, sometime before 1627, and they had ten children. They eventually moved to Boston, where John became a wealthy merchant and ship owner. Mary lived a long, full life, and when she died (around 1679) Mary was one of only two women from the *Mayflower* to leave a will.

Constance married Nicholas Snow and they had twelve children.

Rembrandt van Rijn became one of the greatest artists in European history.

John Billington the younger sadly died around 1627. His younger brother Francis married Christian Eaton in 1630 and they had nine children.

Captain Christopher Jones returned to England with the *Mayflower*. He continued to sail to Europe but died only one year later in 1622, his health probably damaged from the hardships of the *Mayflower* voyage. He was the father of nine children.

Mary's sister Isabella, her husband Roger Chandler, and their four children came to Plymouth around 1630.

Richard More thrived in the New World, living to the ripe old age of eighty-four, married three times and had eight children. He became a well-known sea captain, carrying vital supplies to the new colonies.

John Alden and Priscilla Mullins got married in 1622 and had ten children.

Countless people today can trace their lineage back to one or more of the *Mayflower* passengers.

Of Plymouth Plantation,
. . . *So they lefte that goodly and pleasante citie, which had been their resting place near twelve years; they knew they were pilgrims and looked not much on those things, but lifted up their eyes to ye heavens, their dearest countrie, and quieted their spirits.*
. . . *As one small candle may light a thousand, so the light here kindled hath shone unto many, yea in some sort to our whole nation. As the years went by, their descendants fancied out from England, as far west as the Pacific.*
–William Bradford

People of Interest

Mary Chilton Winslow: Born in Sandwich, Kent, England. She was baptized at St. Peter's Parish on May 31, 1607. In 1620, at the age of thirteen, she was left an orphan at Plymouth. She has been titled the first known woman to step on Plymouth Rock. No record reveals with whom she spent the next few years, but perhaps, for at least part of the time, she was a member of either the Alden or the Standish household. Mary married John Winslow sometime before 1627. He came to Plymouth, a year after the *Mayflower*, on the *Fortune*. Mary lived to bear and raise ten children. Her family moved in the 1650s to Boston, where Mary's husband was a successful merchant and prosperous businessman and ship owner. He died in 1674. Mary died May 1, 1679. Her grave can be found at the Old King's Church Cemetery in Boston, Massachusetts.

James Chilton: Born 1563 in Canterbury, Kent County, England. A tailor in Canterbury, and then lived in Sandwich, Kent, England. He married Susannah Furner, a Leyden Separatist. With his wife and daughter Mary, he left Holland at the age of sixty-four, on the *Mayflower*, for America—leaving two older daughters, Isabella and Engeltgen, behind in Holland. He died on December 8, 1620, while the *Mayflower* lay in the harbor at Provincetown, Cape Cod.

Susannah Furner Chilton: Accompanied by her husband, James Chilton and her youngest daughter, Mary Chilton, on the 1620 voyage aboard the *Mayflower*. She died shortly after arriving at Plymouth.

John Winslow: Married *Mayflower* passenger Mary Chilton. He was born at Droitwich, Worcestershire, on April 16, 1597, and he arrived at Plymouth in 1621 on the *Fortune*. In Boston, around 1655, he became a wealthy merchant and ship owner.

Captain Christopher Jones: Was part owner of the *Mayflower*.

He was a kind and generous man. If it had not been for him, the Pilgrims probably would have all perished during the first winter. He did not dump them ashore and sailed away with winter coming, as many ship captains would have done. He waited until they got settled, letting the weaker ones live on the ship all winter. The Pilgrims lived on the *Mayflower* for three months while shelters were built on the shore. He held a meeting and saw how pale, thin, and woebegone they all looked—half the colony was now under sixteen years old—only four of the mothers were still alive. Nearly half the men were gone, and whole families were missing. With overwhelming challenges, and before they cast themselves into such peril, Captain Jones made them an offer. "We have all had a long, hard, and very sad winter. You have laid half of your number on the hill (a burial ground). Perhaps it would be the wise thing for you to return with me to England. I will take you back." He saw how frail and unhappy they all looked. The Pilgrims thought of the loved ones they had buried. Hardly any family had been spared at least one death.

Mary Chilton told Captain Jones and Governor Carver, "I have no wish to go back to England since all I have is here in Plymouth. I have a good feeling here—I feel loved and protected." So the humble Pilgrims, many who were sick, gave themselves into the hands of God and decided to stay on in New Plymouth. They would miss Captain Jones. He had been good to them. By spring, about half the Pilgrims and sailors were dead. On April 5, 1621, the *Mayflower* departed for England.

Glossary

Adversity: misfortune or troubled state

Adz: an ax-like tool for dressing wood

Almanac: a calendar with astronomical data, weather forecasts, etc.

Anvil: an iron or steel block on which metal objects are hammered into shapes

Asylum: place of safety

Bellows: used for blowing fires

Bid: to be commanded; ordered

Bosun: boatsman

Brevity: to be brief

Burgoo: oatmeal

Cask: A barrel-like container

"Cast off": lift the anchor

Chamber pot: A pot kept near the bed for nighttime bathroom use

Chapbook: a book with chapters

Chaste: pure, decent, modest, simple in style, not ornate

Cipher: to solve arithmetic problems

Coif: a head covering for girls and women made of white linen that covered the hair

Compensation: to make up for

Covenant: an agreement; to promise

Cutlass: a short, heavy, slightly curved sword with a single cutting edge, formerly used by sailors.

Dell: meadow

Dialect: a variety of a spoken language

"Doing naught": doing nothing

Dolt: a stupid person

Doublet: man's close-fitting jacket

Dunes: rounded hill or ridge

Enact: to pass a bill or law

Exploited: to use selfishly for one's own ends

Fathom: a length of six feet, used to measure nautical depth

Foreboding: to have a bad feeling about something

Fortnight: two weeks

Frippery: showy display in dress

Frock: a dress

Gale: a burst of strong wind

Goodwife: term used for lower-status women

Grindstone: a revolving stone dish for sharpening most tools or polishing things

Gruel: a thin soup

Guillotine: an instrument for beheading

Hamlet: a very small village

Hardtack: unleavened bread, large wafers

Hasty pudding: cornmeal mush

Hatch: a door to the 'tween deck or other decks below

Helmsman: one who steers a ship

Herring: a small fish of the North Atlantic

Hewn: chopped or cut with an ax

Hummocky: a low, rounded hill; knoll

Hurly: commotion

Imbecile: fool, idiot

Implement: tool or instrument

Indentured: to be a servant

Laborious: difficult

Lolling: to waste time, aimless activity

Lye: any strong alkaline solution, used in cleaning

"Make bold": to act unafraid, confident, or abrupt

Meerderheid: a festival when Dutch people clean their streets

Mistress: term used for wealthy women

Musket: a type of gun

Ogre: a hideous, cruel man

Ordinance: an order, a statute or regulation

Parchment: the skin of a sheep or goat prepared for writing on.

Pasty: a small meat and vegetable pie held in the hand

Pewter: made from an alloy of tin with lead, bronze, or copper

Pilgrim: someone who goes on a long, long journey

Plymouth Rock: the big rock that came to be known as Plymouth Rock was hallowed after the Pilgrims arrived. Even today it is a symbol of their landing.

Porcelain: translucent ceramic or china

"Preserve better walking": watch your step

Quinsy: early term for tonsillitis

Rations: restricted amount of food

Reflective: serious; thoughtful

Sacrifice: to give up something

Scurvy: a disease resulting from a deficiency in vitamin C found in fruits such as citrus; oranges, lemons, and limes

Sea chest: a large shipping trunk

Seaworthy: able to withstand stormy weather in safety; fit for a sea voyage

Separatist: those who separated themselves because of their beliefs from the oppression of King James and the mandated religion of England—also called Puritans and Pilgrims

Serpent: a snake

Shallop: an open boat fitted with oars, or sails, or both; the shallop on the *Mayflower* had both and was large enough to hold approximately sixteen adult persons

Shoals: a sandbar forming a shallow place

Skein: a quantity of thread or yarn in a coil

Solemnly: seriously

Stock: a wooden frame with holes for confining the ankles or wrists formerly used for punishment

Swell: a wave, especially when long and unbroken, or a series of such waves

Swig: a sip

Temperate: moderate, self-restrained in actions and speech

The Mayflower Compact: promised fair laws and gave the people the right to choose their own leader

Trencher: wooden platter for meat

Trepidation: fear, worry

Unlettered: illiterate

Vanity: being too proud of oneself

Yorkshire pudding: batter baked in meat drippings

Interesting Facts

❖ From England to Holland and then America: why didn't the Separatists give up? To worship freely was more important. Their faith became the foundation of a new nation, the United States of America.

❖ The *Mayflower* may have flown pennants as well as a flag of the cross of Saint George, a red cross on white background. Saint George is the patron saint of England. Ships like the *Mayflower* were designed to sail before the wind. By adjusting and moving the whipstaff to move the rudder, the pilot navigated, or conned, the ship. There were fifty-five live, or working, lines on the *Mayflower* used to adjust the sails. All the sailors were kept very busy. In a storm, sails were clewed up and then furled so that they would not hold wind, and the ship was allowed to drift.

❖ Because no one kept journals, the Pilgrims handed down stories and they became myths. William Bradford wrote important information, which became the book *Of Plymouth Plantation.* His vast journal was lost for many years, only turning up again in the 1850s in England.

❖ William Bradford was mayor of Plymouth, Massachusetts five times and died at the age of sixty-five. He said, "Let the right hand of Lord awake," and "What our fathers with so much difficulty attained, do not basely relinquish." (Latin)

❖ James Neil, 1731 *History of Plymouth* likened the Pilgrims to the flower chamomile: "The more it is trodden down, the more it grows."

❖ "Sweet are the uses of adversity," engraved on Mary's locket, comes from Shakespeare's play, *As You Like It*. The remainder of the quote is, "Which, like a toad, though ugly and venomous, wears yet a precious jewel in its head."

❖ The ship's passengers did not think they were sailing into history. They gave no thought to being in future history books.

❖ Mary Chilton's rag doll can be seen today in the Pilgrim Hall Museum. It is almost four hundred years old. Cloth does not weather the years very well, so it is amazing that this precious treasure from the past still exists today, a tangible reminder of the very real girl who crossed the Atlantic on the *Mayflower*.

Special notes following the arrival of the *Mayflower* at Plymouth, Massachusetts:

- ❖ The *Mayflower* first spotted land at Plymouth, Massachusetts on the morning of December 20, 1620.

- ❖ There came a day when only six or seven were well enough to hunt for food, care for the sick, and bury the dead. Every few days, another Pilgrim would die. Those who were still alive were afraid to have so many graves showing. They feared the Indians would overtake them. Soon the Indians became their friends. Before long, the Indians showed them how to plant and get food from wilderness and the sea. More would have starved without the help of the friendly Indians.

- ❖ By the first year, the settlers made a fairly sturdy alliance with the Indians.

- ❖ History has shown that the Pilgrim leaders had good reason to worry about their survival. Before the next harvest was gathered, everyone in the colony knew what starvation was like. The men were weary with weakness as they tried to keep at their jobs. Their clothing hung on them in tatters like rags on a scarecrow, but somehow the Pilgrims managed to survive.

- ❖ By 1627, over 150 people lived in Plymouth. Back in England, William Shakespeare published his plays while Rembrandt van Rijn was painting in Holland.

- ❖ Scrooby—80 miles west of Alford, England—the place from which the Separatists left.

Notes from the Author

The purpose of this book is to tell the story of young Mary Chilton, her family, and friends. The adventures of Mary begin the year she was born, in 1607. It can only be told well from a larger perspective with a brave group of humble people who set out in 1620 for a new life in a land that was unknown to them. Readers often ask if this story is true. *Mary of the Mayflower* is historical fiction—a work of the imagination, but the most important part of it is true.

Much has been written in greater detail that will support these historical facts. I hope that through the life of young Mary, each reader will have new insight and a desire to learn more about our founding fathers and mothers.

With the encouragement of my father, Stanley Walker Stevenson, and his tireless research, I began this journey. After my own research and visits to Plymouth Plantation in Plymouth, Massachusetts, I have been inspired to write this story about my ancestor, Mary Chilton. My hope is to bring both balance and perspective to Mary Chilton's story. *Mary of the Mayflower* captures this American heroine's life in all its complexity.

You will discover more by going on a rewarding trip to Plymouth, Massachusetts, where you can experience an authentic 1620 simulation of how life was then. Also, you can step onto the *Mayflower II* and explore the ship that rests in the Plymouth Harbor. It will give you a new understanding of freedom and thanksgiving.

Before history is written in books, it is written in courage. Our country's history is a spiritual, stirring saga. Liberty costs a great deal. It is our heritage and privilege to protect it for the next generation.

A Few Sources on Mary Chilton's Story

The following traditional anecdote has always been regarded as correct among the Chilton descendants: The *Mayflower* having arrived in the harbor of Plymouth, Massachusetts, Mary Chilton was permitted to enter the landing boat as she looked forward, exclaiming, "I will be the first to step on that Rock." Accordingly, when the boat approached, Mary Chilton was permitted to be the first from that boat who appeared on that rock, and thus her claim was established.

A well-known story originated in a talk given in the eighteenth century at Plymouth's Old Colony Club that at age ninety-five, Elder Faunce was driven to town in an open wagon from Eel River and taken to Plymouth Rock. He told the people gathered there how he had talked to John Howland and his wife, John Alden, Giles Hopkins, George Soule, Francis Cooke and his son John, and Mrs. Cushman. All of these, he said, told him that it was upon that rock that they had stepped ashore, and John Winslow's wife, Mary (Chilton), had come there on her seventy-fifth birthday and laughed as she stepped on the rock and said she was the first woman to have stepped on it. This story, relayed to posterity verbally by one who claimed to hear it from a person who had been in Elder Faunce's audience that day, is as far back as we can go to authenticate that what we today call Plymouth Rock was in fact the first land at Plymouth touched by the *Mayflower* passengers. (See Eugene Aubrey Stratton, *Plymouth Colony: Its History and People, 1620–1691*, 1986.)

Another source, although not the earliest form in which I have found it is as follows: "Mary Chilton was the first European Female that landed on the North America shore; she came over with her father and mother and other adventurers to this new settlement. One thing worthy of notice is that her curiosity of being the first on the American Strand prompted her, like a young Heroine, to leap

193

out of the boat and wade ashore." (Annie Arnoux Haxtun, *Signers of the Mayflower Compact*, 1897).

The tradition also traces back to Mrs. Ann Taylor-Winslow through other channels. In the enlarged edition of *History of the Town of Plymouth*, by James Thacher, 1835, is an extended footnote on the Boston Winslows, furnished by a descendant. This says: "The tradition of the family, confirmed by a writing at the death of Ann Taylor, in 1773, is, that Mary Chilton 'was the first female who set her foot on the American shore.'"

A third channel leads back both to Madam Ann Winslow and to her cousins the Lathams, but was not reduced to writing, as far as I have found, until 1853. Hon. Beza Hayward, H.C. 1772, teaching school in Milton, became acquainted with the widow Ann Taylor, then ninety-four years old, and claiming, like himself, to be descended from Mary Chilton. This elderly lady communicated to him the following family tradition, which he often related in our presence, as nearly as I can now recollect, in the following words: "Mary Chilton, when going ashore in the boat, said she would be the first to land, jumped out, and wetting her feet, ran to the shore." (William Shaw Russell, *Pilgrim Memorials and Guide to Plymouth*, 1855.)

The earliest I have found the story in print is in 1815, in *"Notes on Plymouth,"* attributed to Samuel Davis: "There is a tradition as to the person who first leaped upon the rock, when the families came on shore, December 11, 1620: it is said to have been a young woman, Mary Chilton. This information comes from a source so correct as induces us to admit it; and it is a very probable circumstance, from the natural impatience of a young person, or any other, after a long confinement on shipboard, to reach the land, and to escape from the crowded boat. We leave it, therefore, as we find it, in the hand of history and the fine arts."

Notes of History

In 1620, the Pilgrims sailed to America in order to escape religious and political persecution and establish a settlement where they could love and worship in a way that they defined as freedom of expression, thoughts, and religion.

In their homeland of England, under the reign of King James I, the Church of England was very powerful. Anyone who did not follow the established religion or cooperate with the king's wishes faced persecution in the form of arrest, imprisonment, fines, and other types of official harassment, even death.

A group of people called Puritans questioned the church's power, and a growing faction of them began to condemn the church as corrupt and unlawful. They were scorned by the king, because their questioning threatened his authority as well as that of the church. Some of them began to meet in secret. They were known as Separatists, because they wanted to separate themselves entirely from the teachings of the church. When the king found out about their secret meetings, some Separatists were sentenced to jail. In 1607, a group of them decided they could no longer live in a country where religion was forced on people under threat of arrest.

For fear of their livelihoods as well as their lives, the Separatists decided to move to Leyden, Holland, where they could live and worship freely. But life in Holland was hard economically, and they felt extremely alone in this new land. They were also worried that their children would forget how to speak English or that they would marry the Dutch, or become soldiers and sailors for the country of Holland.

They decided to immigrate to the New World. These Separatists came to be known as Pilgrims. They were led by William Brewster, a fine leader, and another wise young man, William Bradford. Another English colony had already been established in Jamestown, Virginia, in 1607, and they were ready to create another new colony in Northern Virginia.

In London, some businessmen, the Merchant Adventurers, agreed to sponsor their voyage. In exchange for financial backing by the London group, the Pilgrims promised to work for the next seven years to pay off their debts. They would become indentured servants to this coalition of merchants, who hoped to gain a great profit from their chartered colony. In England they were provided with a small wooden ship named the *Mayflower* and some supplies to help the Pilgrims survive their first months in the wilderness of America.

On Wednesday, September 6, 1620, 102 courageous people, including thirty-four children, crowded onto the ship and set off to create a colony of their own. About forty of them were going for religious reasons—they were the Pilgrims (though they liked to call themselves Saints.) Others came because they couldn't find work in England, and still others simply for the adventure.

The journey was longer than expected and difficult. There was little to eat except for salted beef and pork, dry biscuits, and also some cheese, peas, and beans from Holland. But most of the food spoiled quickly and the barreled water was not safe to drink. Many of the passengers were extremely sick, and two (including one sailor) died during the grueling journey. After more than two months, the Pilgrims arrived at what is now Cape Cod, Massachusetts. Since they had been planning to settle in Virginia Colony, it was clear that they had gone a great distance off course.

Cape Cod looked to be a rocky and ominous land. After determining to explore farther, the Pilgrims sailed inland to the less dangerous shores of Plymouth, which had been discovered and named six years earlier by Captain John Smith. On December 21, 1620, the Pilgrims finally came ashore. Generations tell of the legend that Mary Chilton was the first to step onto Plymouth Rock, which loomed out of the two-and-a-half-mile sandy beach.

The first few months in Plymouth were cold and harsh for the Pilgrims. Coming to this foreign land in the dead of winter was probably the wrong thing to do. The Pilgrims arrived with no shelter, no medical care, and very few provisions. Because houses needed to be built, many of them spent most of the winter living aboard the ship. Illness swept through the tiny community, and more than half the Pilgrims died during that first winter. Most passed away from starvation and scurvy, while others died from pneumonia, fevers, and other diseases. While the Pilgrims did use medicinal herbs, there was no medicine that could cure the out-of-control diseases that were killing them.

The Pilgrims had agreed to elect John Carver to be their first governor, but he did not survive the long winter. William Bradford was then elected to take his place. He and the other leaders of the group created a document called the *Mayflower* Compact, signed by all of the men in the new colony. Annual elections were held for a governor and assistants, who would draft fair laws for all to follow. While America's struggle for independence was over 150 years away, the early seeds of self-government were sown by the forward-thinking Pilgrims.

Very soon after the Plymouth colonists arrived, they came into contact with the Indian people. Some of the local tribes, like the various Wampanoag groups, were friendly toward the Pilgrims. The Wampanoag had been trading furs with European traders for years before the *Mayflower* landed, but the Pilgrim passengers were the first Europeans to settle permanently on Wampanoag land.

On March 16, 1621, months after their arrival, the Pilgrims met an Abenaki Indian named Samoset who spoke English and told them all about the neighboring Indian tribes. He also introduced them to another Indian named Tisquantum, or Squanto, the only surviving Patuxet native of Plymouth. He became their loyal friend and stayed near the Pilgrims for the rest of his life. When spring came and the Pilgrims were able to plant their first crops, Squanto introduced them to maize (Indian corn). He also taught the Pilgrims how to fish and where to find the best places to hunt for deer and turkey. While some of the English crops like beans and wheat did not grow very well in the rocky New England soil, maize seemed to thrive. The Pilgrims traded their extra corn to the Indians for beaver pelts. These furs were then sent to England to help pay off their debts.

There were other tribes, like the Gayhead and the Narrangansetts, who were not as kind to the Pilgrims, and Captain Miles Standish helped form a militia, providing security for the fledgling community.

That October, the surviving Pilgrims (only about fifty) celebrated the first Thanksgiving. It lasted three days, and they invited members of the Wampanoag tribe to join them for the celebrated feast. They ate wild turkey, deer, meat pies, duck, fresh fish, vegetables from the Pilgrims' gardens, corn, and wild berries and nuts. The Pilgrims that survived had much to be thankful for. Without the help of Squanto and their Indian neighbors, they would not have lived through their first year. They also signed an official peace treaty with the Wampanoag chief, Massasoit. Later, the British would try to take advantage of the Pilgrims' new allies and attempt to force them to move away from their ancestral lands, but in the end this did not happen.

For the next few years, the hardy Pilgrims were almost isolated in their new settlement. Their population grew slowly. Every so often, ships would arrive from England with some new immigrants. For the most part, though, the Pilgrims were on their own to fend for themselves.

The company of London never did make a profit from the Pilgrims. It was too hard to exert complete control over colonies that were so far away. Plymouth was now all but independent, although the king of England still had final jurisdiction over their activities. In reality, the Pilgrims were a self-governing community; however, their fight for independence was only just beginning.

Mary became the wife of Governor Winslow's brother, John, sometime before 1627, after he arrived on the *Fortune* in 1621. They had ten children and owned a large, elegantly furnished home, gardens, acreage, stables, and two small cargo boats. She died around 1679, making a small M for a signature on her will that left silver pieces, pewter, and much clothing to her heirs. Her tombstone in the tiny Granary Burying Grounds beside King's Chapel, now in Boston's business section, bears the Winslow coat of arms.

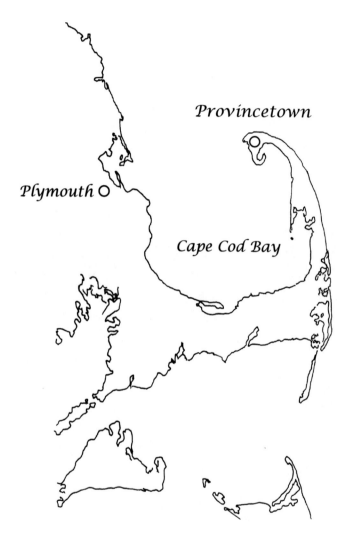

Diane Stevenson Stone

Provincetown

Plymouth ○

Cape Cod Bay

Atlantic Ocean

EARLY NEW ENGLAND

The Mayflower *was not a passenger ship, but a cargo ship. About ninety feet long, it was made to transport things like cloth and barrels of wine.*

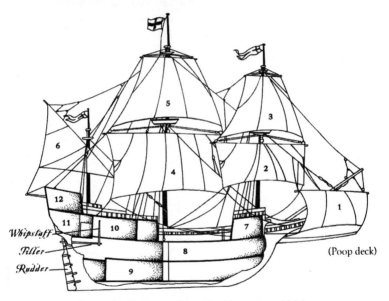

Diagram of the Mayflower with her sails and important areas labeled.

1. SPRITSAIL
2. FORECOURSE
3. FORE-TOPSAIL
4. MAIN COURSE
5. MAIN-TOPSAIL.
6. MIZZEN SAIL
7. FO'C'SLE
   This is where meals were cooked for the crew.
8. 'TWEEN DECKS
   This is where the passengers lived during the journey.

9. HOLD
   This is where food, drink, tools, and supplies were stored.
10. STEERAGE
    This is where the helmsman steered the ship by moving the whipstaff, the long lever that moves the tiller, which moves the rudder. An officer on the deck above steerage gave the orders.
11. GREAT CABIN
    This is where the ship's master, some of the officers, and the ship's apprentice slept.
12. ROUND HOUSE
    This is the chartroom from which the master directed the ship's course.

PASSENGERS ON THE MAYFLOWER

"The names of those which came over first, in the year 1620, and were by the blessing of God the first beginners and in a sort the foundation of all the Plantations and Colonies in New England; and their families."

John Carver and Katherine, his wife. Desire Minter and two manservants, *John Howland*, Roger Wilder. William Latham, a boy. A maidservant and a child that was put to John Carver called Jasper More.

William Brewster and Mary, his wife; their two sons, **Love** and **Wrestling**. A boy that was put to him called **Richard More**, and his sister, Mary. The rest of the Brewster's children were left behind but came later.

Edward Winslow and Elizabeth, his wife. Two manservants called *George Soule* and Elias Story; also, a little girl was put to him called Ellen, the sister of Richard More.

William Bradford and his wife, Dorothy. The Bradfords had one son who remained behind but came on a later ship.

Isaac Allerton and his wife, Mary, and their three children, **Bartholomew, Remember**, and **Mary**. And a servant boy John Hooke.

Samuel Fuller and a servant called William Button. Samuel Fuller's wife and their child came afterwards.

John Crackstone and his son, **John Crackstone**.

Captain Myles Standish and Rose, his wife.

Christopher Martin and his wife, and two servants, Solomon Prower and John Langmore.

William Mullins, his wife Alice, and their two children, Joseph and **Priscilla**; as well as a servant, Robert Carter.

William White and his wife, **Susanna**, and their son, **Resolved**, and a son born aboard ship, called **Peregrine**. Also, two servants named William Holbeck and Edward Thompson.

Stephen Hopkins and Elizabeth, his wife, and their two children, **Damaris** and **Oceanus**; the latter was born at sea. Also, Stephen Hopkins' children from his first marriage, **Giles** and **Constance**. And two servants called *Edward Doty* and *Edward Lester*.

Richard Warren. His wife and children were left behind but came later.

John Billington and his wife Elinor, and their two sons, **John** and **Francis**.

Edward Tilley and Ann, his wife, and two children that were their cousins **Henry Sampson** and **Humility Cooper**.

Names in *italic* indicate the signers of the Mayflower Compact; names in **bold** letters indicate those who survived the first year.

John Tilley and his wife, and **Elizabeth**, their daughter.

Francis Cooke and his son, **John**. Francis Cooke's wife and other children came afterwards.

Thomas Rogers and **Joseph**, his son; his other children came afterwards.

Thomas Tinker, his wife, and a son.

John Rigdale and his wife, Alice.

James Chilton, his wife, and their daughter, **Mary**. Their other daughter, who was married, came later.

Edward Fuller, his wife and **Samuel**, their son.

John Turner and two sons. He had a daughter who came some years later to Salem.

Francis Eaton and Sarah, his wife, and **Samuel**, their son, a young child.

Moses Fletcher. His wife, Sarah, and his children remained in Holland.

Digory Priest. His wife, Sarah, and children stayed behind in Holland. Sarah, with the knowledge of her husband's death, married Godbert Godbertson. The family came to New Plymouth in 1623.

John Goodman.

Thomas Williams, Edmund Margesson, Peter Browne, Richard Britteridge, Richard Clarke, Richard Gardiner, Gilbert Winslow.

John Alden was hired as a cooper at Southampton where the ship was supplied. Left to his own liking to go or stay, he decided to stay and married in New Plymouth.

John Allerton and *Thomas English* were both hired. The latter to master a shallop in the new colony; the other was reputed as one of the company but was to go back (being a seaman) for the help of others behind. However, they both died before the ship returned.

There were also two other seamen hired to stay a year in the colony; William Trevor and one Ely, but when their time was out they both returned to England.

ADAPTED FROM:
William Bradford
Of Plymouth Plantation 1620-1647
Samuel Eliot Morison, editor
1970 (Alfred A. Knopf, New York)

Plimoth Plantation
P.O. Box 1620
Plymouth, MA 02362
(508) 746-1622 x 8352 (Mail Order)
(800) 262-9356 x 8352 (Mail Order)
www.plimoth.org

Last Will & Testament
of Mary Chilton Winslow

"In the name of God Amen the thirty first day of July in the yeare of our Lord one thousand Six hundred seventy Six I Mary Winslow of Boston in New England widdow being weake of Body but of Sound and perfect memory praysed be almighty God for the same Knowing the uncertainty of this present life and being desirous to settle that outward Estate the Lord hath Lent me. I doe make this my last will and Testamt in manner and forme following (that is to say) First and principally I commend my Soule into the hands of Almighty God my Creator hopeing to receive full pardon and remission of all my sins; and salvation through the alone merrits of Jesus Christ my redeemer: And my body to the Earth to be buried in Such Decent manner as to my Executor hereafter named shall be thought meet and convenient and as touching such worldly Estate as the Lord hath Lent me my will and meaneing is the same shall be imployed and bestowed as hereafter in and by this my Will is Exprest.

"Imps I doe hereby revoake renounce and make voide all Wills by me formerly made and declaire and apoint this my Last Will and Testamt Item I will that all the Debts that I Justly owe to any manner of person or persons whatsoever shall be well and truly paid or ordained to be paid in convenient time after my decease by my executor hereafter named—Item I give and bequeath unto my Sone John Winslow my great Square Table Item I give and bequeath unto my Daughter Sarah Middlecott my Best gowne and Pettecoat and my silver beare bowle and to each of her children a Silver Cup with an handle: Also I give unto my grandchild William Paine my Great silver tankard: Item I give unto my Daughter Susanna Latham my long Table: Six Joyned Stooles and my great Cupboard: a bedstead Bedd and furniture there unto belonging that is in the chamber over the room where I now Lye; my small silver Tankard: Six Silver Spoones, a case of bottles with all my wearing apparell: (except onely what I have hereby bequeathed unto my Daughter Meddlecott & my Grandchild Susanna Latham: Item I give and bequeath unto my Grandchild Ann Gray that trunke of linnin that I have alreddy delivered to her and is in her possession and also one Bedstead, Bedd boulster and Pillows that are in the Chamber over the Hall: Also the sume of ten pounds in mony to be paid unto her within six months next after my decease: Also my will is that my Executor shall pay foure pounds in mony pr ann for three yeares unto Mrs Tappin out of the Intrest of my mony now in Goodman Cleares hands for and toward the maintenance of the said Ann Gray according to my agreemt with Mrs Tappin: Item I give and bequeath unto Mary Winslow Daughter of my sone Edward Winslow my largest Silver Cupp with two handles: and unto Sarah Daughter of the said Edward my lesser Silver cupp with two handles: Also I give unto my Said Sone Edwards Children Six Silver Spoones to be divided between them: Item I give and bequeath unto my grandchild Parnell Winslow the Sume of five pounds in mony to be improved by my Executor untill he come of age: and then paid unto him with the improvemt. Item I give & bequeath unto My grandchild Chilton Latham the sum of five pounds in mony to be improved for him untill he come of age and then paid to him with the improvemt. Item my will is that the rest of my spoones be divided among my grandchildren according to the discression of My Daughter Middlecott: Item I give unto my Grandchild Mercy Harris my White rugg: Item I give unto my Grandchild Mary Pollard forty shillings in mony. Item I give unto my grandchild Susanna Latham my Petty

Coate with the silke Lace: Item I give unto Mary Winslow Daughter of my Sone Joseph Winslow the Sume of twenty pounds in mony to be paid out of the sumy my said Sone Joseph now owes to be improved by my Executor for the said Mary and paid unto her when she shall attaine the Age of eighteene yeares or day of Marriage which of them shall first happen Item I give and bequeath the full remainder of my estate whatsoever it is or whatsoever it may be found unto my children Namely John Winslow Edward Winslow Joseph Winslow Samuell Winslow: Susanna Latham and Sarah Middlecott to be equally divided betweene them Item I doe hereby nominate constitute authorize and appoint my trusty friend Mr William Tailer of Boston aforesd merchant the Sole Executor of this my last Will and testamt: In witness whereof I the said Mary Winslow have hereunto set my hand and Seale the daye and yeare first above written

"Memorandum I do hereby also Give and bequeath unto Mr Thomas Thacher paster of the third Church in Boston the Sume of five pounds in mony to be pd convenient time after my decease by my Executr

Mary Winslow

M her marke (Seal)

The inventory of the goods of Mary Chilton Winslow, deceased 1679

Note: inventories are valued in pounds (L), shillings (s) and pence (d). There were 12 pence (or pennies) to a shilling and 20 shillings to a pound.

To 1.1. Silver beer Boule. 3L. Two Silver Cups. 4L10.

To .1. small Silver Tankard at 4L.10. twelve Silver Spoons .6L

To .1. silver caudle Cup with two eares

To .1. small silver Cup at .10s. one case with 9 bottles 12s.

To .1. silke gowne and petticoate at

To .1. gowne .6. petticoats .1. pair. body's .1. mantle .1. pair Stockins

To .1. Bed and boulster with fflocks and ffeathers

To .1. close bedsteed .2. coverlits & .2. old blankets .1. old Rugg .1.

To .2. Leather Chaires at 10s. one ffeather Bed at 4L.5

To .11. old Sheets at .35s. one diaper Table Cloth .10s.

To .3. old ffustian wastcoats at

To .22. old Napkins .7s. Six Towels .2s.

To .11. pillowbeers

To .6. Shifts at

To .6. white Aprons .18s. Seven neck handkercheifs 10/6

To .17. Linnen Caps 8s.6. ffourteen headbands .6s.

To .3. Pocket handkercheifs. 18d. one Trunke .8s.

To .1. old Chest 4s. one round Table. 10s.

To .1. small cupboard 4s. one small Trunke. 18d

To .1. pr. of small Andirons .4/6. one old warmingpan 3/6

To .2. small brass kettles .15s. one small Iron pot & hookes .6/6

To .1. gridiron .12d. one great wicker chair .7/6

To .1. Close Stoole and a pan

To .1. great elbow chaire .2/6. one brass candlestick. 15d.

To .1 voyder .18d. one Iron fender. 12d

To .1. old bedsteed

To .3. great pewter dishes and .20. small peices of pewtr

In debts by bills standing out

To one halfe of the house which was formerly mr Joseph Winslows

To .1. Spit .2/6. one pr brass Scales .4/6

At Mr John Winslow's House

To .1. Long table and .6. joint Stooles at

To .1. pr. small brass Andirons

To .1. old cupboard .7s. one pothanger Iron Skillet and one pa of

To .9. Leather Chairs .36s. one Bedsteed .6s

To .1. standing cupboard .20s. one great Chest .10s.

To .1. small table .8s. two small bedsteeds .2s.

To .3. chaires without Leathers .6s. one pr ffire Irons .3/6.

To .1. Scotch blanket .5s. one pr old striped stuffe curtains

To .1. woosted Rugg .18s. one small ffeather pillow .3s.

To .12. ps. of pewter and .6. plates

To .1. old Trunks

Total

Reading Group Guide

1. What is it about the Pilgrims that gave them the desire and drive to sacrifice everything and move from England to Holland and finally across the sea to unknown lands?

2. Mary has the heartbreaking experience of leaving her dearest friends, family, and even her dear cat "Master Albert." Can you relate to her emotions? How would it make you feel?

3. Have you ever been bullied? If you were on a ship with few places to hide, how would you handle the unexpected and disturbing behavior of the Billington boys?

4. The Chilton family chooses to leave their home in England under frightening and life-threatening circumstances for religious freedom. What would you and your family do if you had to make such a choice? Is there anything you would be willing to sacrifice everything for?

5. How do Mary, Goodwife Chilton, and some of the other women exhibit strength and courage in a time during which women had no voice?

6. How does Mary find the strength to carry on in the midst of hunger, cold, illness, and dangers that occurred during the ship's voyage?

7. If you were a passenger on the *Mayflower* among strangers and people who had different beliefs, sharing a small space, what are some ways you could build friendships with others?

8. Even though Mary never knew her grandmother, what is it that makes Mary feel so close to her? What do you know and love about your grandmother or grandfather?

9. As you consider the events that took place in the story, was there any part that you especially liked? Are there lessons you learned that will stay with you in your own life?

10. Mary sometimes feels like her life is difficult until she learns about the experiences of others (like the More children being sent away from their mother and Johnny being a poor orphan). Have you ever had a time when you realized that your troubles weren't as hard as someone else's?

11. If you, like the Chilton family, had to leave everything behind, and you could only take what you could carry and wear, what are some of the things you would take with you, and why?

12. Aside from the hard times, what are some happy and positive things Mary experiences?

Author Diane Stevenson Stone

As a member of the Mayflower Society, Diane enjoys speaking at Mayflower colonies and schools across the country.

She was delighted to find the actual grave site of her ancestor, Mary Chilton Winslow, at the old King's Chapel located in the center of Boston, Massachusetts.

About the Author/Illustrator

Diane Stevenson Stone's personal story started in Los Angeles, California, and has taken her around the world from Boston, Massachusetts, to French Polynesia; to Glendale and subsequently Modesto, California; through France and England; and finally back to California's central coast in Pebble Beach, where she now resides with her husband, Tom. Her works of art have been exhibited at the American Embassy in Paris, France, where she studied at the École des Beaux-Arts. Her artwork has also been featured in galleries from Papeete, Tahiti, to Carmel-by-the-Sea, California, though she claims her eight children as her very finest works of art. Diane's talent for storytelling is enjoyed by all, but especially by her thirty grandchildren. More recently, she has served as chair of the Leadership Council for the Museum of Art at Brigham Young University. Her first book, *A Big Family Reunion With Sarah Lucy*, is also available through Amazon.

Diane has often wondered about her forefathers. How did they live their lives? What were their dreams? What did they think of heaven and earth? Every story ever told is a family story, and this is how her book came to be. Diane explains, "My father, Stanley Walker Stevenson, researched numerous ancestors who made that treacherous journey on the *Mayflower* to the New World. Before he died, he asked me if I would write a story about our brave young progenitor, Mary Chilton. In doing so, I have gained a deeper appreciation for the hopes and dreams of those early Pilgrims and the struggles they endured in creating the initial foundation for the United States of America." She hopes that each reader of Mary's story will likewise be touched and inspired to expand and enhance the cherished freedoms of our beloved America.

CPSIA information can be obtained at www.ICGtesting.com
Printed in the USA
LVOW07*2239220216

476229LV00001B/2/P